flowers FROM death

ZENNA ROSE

Cover Design: Covers by Jules

Ever since the accident that shattered my world and killed my best friend, I've yearned for a new life.

Columbia University offers just that. Freedom. A fresh start. A chance to be normal for once.

But it soon becomes clear that I didn't come here alone.

The nightmare starts out with small gestures. Little gifts. All of them accompanied by notes in a slanted handwriting that I almost—but don't quite—recognize.

And then the murders begin.

Someone is following me, watching me, and ensuring that nobody who lays a finger on my body is allowed to live.

Will I ever get away from my faceless stalker?

Am I sure that I want to get away?

And why am I somehow sure that the answers lie in my past... a past that I barely remember?

A past with a boy who, for the last three miserable years, I believed to be dead?

content warning

Flowers From Death is a dark romance.

It does contain content and situations that could be triggering to some readers such as dub/con, murder, stalking, sexual assault, and drugs.

Please check my website for a list of all triggers before reading.

For a full list of triggers please see my website.

www.zennarosebooks.com

chapter one

"Okay. Here's what *I* think." Tanya taps her fingernail, sea-green and perfectly manicured, against the edge of the restaurant table.

I suppress a groan. That tone—not to mention the look in her keen brown eyes—is never a good sign. Tanya, as much as I love her, is *always* saying what she thinks—and when she takes the time to preface her opinion with a statement like this, it means that she knows I'm not going to be happy about it.

"I think—and hear me out—that you're getting too worked up about all this. Caught up in your own head, you know? You're stressed as hell about starting college, about the bullshit with Andrew…"

This time, I can't keep myself from sighing.

"Come on, babe." She shoots me a half-smile, and its message is clear: *I feel for you, but this shit is getting pretty old, don't you think?* "He's not *that* bad. I mean, aside from how messed up the whole arranged marriage stuff might be on principle—at least he's hot, y'know?"

I don't know if I'd go that far. Andrew Clark is an Abercrombie boy through and through. Tall, blonde, athletic, and boasting a tan that's admittedly impressive for someone born and raised in Chicago. Appealing to someone like Tanya, maybe. But I wouldn't look twice at him if not for what she calls 'the whole arranged marriage stuff.' It's not quite as vulgar as she makes it sound—my parents haven't even told me outright that they want me to marry into the Clark family —but it's pretty damn obvious.

"But anyway," Tanya continues, "that's why you're having these nightmares. Feeling all paranoid like this. That's pretty much basic psychology."

"Dreams," I correct her automatically. "Not nightmares."

"Well, they sure *sound* like nightmares."

Maybe so—but if they do, it's because I'm not describing them well. The visions that have filled my nights for the past few weeks may be haunted with mist and shadows, but they're also strangely comforting, in a way.

Even if they do revolve around a boy who's been dead for three years.

I should be over it by now. That's what everyone thinks, even if they won't say it to my face. Nobody wants to tell a girl that she should stop moping about the car crash that killed her best friend—especially if the girl in question was rendered comatose in the same accident, just a hair's breadth away from losing her own life. But I know that they talk about it behind my back. My family, my friends, even Andrew. They want me to move on.

But how can anyone move on from someone like Nyx?

Nicholas Caballero. Nyx to his friends—a.k.a. me. I don't remember him being close to anyone else. He wasn't a super social guy. Everything about him, from his steel-gray eyes to his brooding demeanor, tended to put people on edge. But I knew him better than anyone. I'm sure of that much, even if the coma-induced amnesia robbed me of the details of our friendship. I know that I saw through that cold exterior, straight to his core, which burned with the white-hot flame of pure passion.

Until the crash extinguished it.

"Delaney. You're drifting again."

Tanya's voice startles me back to the present. She's watching me with pursed lips, tugging at the tips of her long dark curls.

"Sorry. Just—"

"A lot on your mind," she finishes for me. "And a lot on your plate—literally and figuratively. You haven't eaten at all."

Sure enough, the chicken Caesar salad on my plate sits untouched. How long have we been sitting here? Half an hour? More? I pick up my fork and prod at the parmesan-studded leaves, not quite able to bring myself to take a bite.

"Look," Tanya sighs. "Try to look on the bright side, yeah? You're about to leave all of this behind. You've had one hell of a string of bad luck, but people at Columbia aren't going to know that. They aren't going to know about—well, about Daniel."

And there it is. The other thing weighing on me, the one that even Tanya is a little scared to mention. The car crash that killed Nyx may be years in the past, but it hasn't even been six months since Daniel died. Murdered, most likely, though the police never managed to pin down any real suspects.

Everyone thinks that I was traumatized by losing him. Why wouldn't they? We were the hottest couple at prom, totally dominating the dance floor, earning dozens of envious stares over the course of the night. Nobody, not even Tanya, knows about what happened afterwards. How he showed his true colors, how I had to almost physically fight him off of me in the backseat of his car.

In a morbid way, Daniel's death was almost a relief.

But then the fucking gifts kept coming.

I'd assumed they were from him. We hadn't been dating, not formally, but he'd been flirting with me all year long, so it made sense that he'd be the one sending me packages with no return address. Black roses, dark chocolate, earrings studded with garnet and obsidian... weird stuff, for sure, but I brushed it off. Daniel had always been kind of intense. It wasn't a big deal.

Until it was.

Because Daniel has been dead for months, and I got a package as recently as this morning. A sprig of belladonna, my favorite flower, and a note in unfamiliar handwriting:

Careful now. Remember that the most beautiful things are often the most deadly.

Yeah, that would be enough to freak anyone out.

Which is why I invited Tanya to lunch today—but she's not nearly as perturbed as I am by the news. For someone as practical-minded as her, a weird stalker is nothing that a burglar alarm and a baseball bat can't solve. Creepy dreams, on the other hand, could be much worse. They could indicate that there is something profoundly and irrevocably fucked up about the psyche of Delaney Miller.

Am I fucked up?

Probably. After the shit I've been through, it's hard not to be.

But the dreams aren't the problem, whatever Tanya

thinks. I *know* that they aren't, know it in the exact sort of intuitive, intangible way that she would never understand.

"Sorry," she mutters, glancing down. "I shouldn't have brought him up."

It takes me a moment to remember who she's talking about—between Nyx, Daniel, and Andrew, I've got no shortage of unfortunate history when it comes to guys.

"It's okay. And you're right—it'll be nice to get out of here."

"Tell me about it." Her voice grows dreamy. "Sunny days, white sand beaches... I can practically smell the salt water. Or, um, New York City, in your case," she adds quickly. "Which is also totally cool. Like... museums! And Broadway!"

I let out a thin chuckle. "Yeah, I don't know if I'm going to have much time for musical theatre. Columbia's no joke. Pre-law especially."

Tanya shakes her head in bemused disbelief, curls bouncing. "Babe, you're a madwoman. I can't imagine subjecting myself to a prison like that."

"Can't be more of a prison than it is here," I point out, trying and failing to spear a crouton—it breaks to pieces under the tines of my fork.

"Because of Andrew?" Her voice lowers to a near-whisper. "Or because of the stalker?"

"Both, I guess. But mostly because of my parents."

"Oh. Right." Tanya's lips press into a thin line. "You know... you can't really blame them, though, can you? If I had a daughter who went through as much shit as you have, I'd be pretty overprotective, too."

I guess she's right, but that doesn't make my situation any less suffocating. Things have been pretty bad ever since the coma, but they amped up like crazy after Daniel was found dead. My parents wouldn't even let me talk to anyone other than the police for the first couple of weeks—and there was a *lot* of talking to the police, no matter how much I insisted that I didn't know a single thing. Last I saw of him, he was flipping me off out the driver's side window as he drove away, leaving me stranded in a public park at one o'clock in the morning. Whatever happened between then and the discovery of his mangled body is anyone's guess.

"It's not that I blame them, exactly," I say, shrugging under the weight of Tanya's questioning stare. "I just wish they would understand that I can take care of myself."

"*Can* you take care of yourself?"

"Tanya. Seriously?"

"I don't know!" She tosses her napkin onto her own empty plate with a good deal more aggression than necessary. "Look at you—you aren't even *eating*. And NYC is a pretty scary place. Do you know how many murders happen there every year?"

"Chicago's rate is higher. Like, way higher."

"But you aren't *alone* here! You have your parents, and you have me. Hell, I hate to say it, but you even have Andrew."

"I'd take a murderer over Andrew any day of the week."

It's half a joke, but Tanya's darkened expression shows just how unamused she is. "Don't say shit like that."

"Okay, okay. I'm sorry. I hear you. I'm eating, see?" I scoop up a heaping forkful of salad and stuff it in my mouth. The lettuce has wilted under the Caesar dressing after sitting untouched for so long, but it's still flavorful enough—my stomach, seemingly remembering its purpose, lets out an eager growl.

"Good." Tanya's expression is still stern, but her voice softens slightly. "It's not that I don't trust you, or that I think you're irresponsible—you know that, right?"

"I know."

"Okay. Good."

But, as I continue to nibble at my food, I realize that I'm not so sure. I'm tired of the way that everyone looks at me, Tanya included. A little bit pitying, a little bit cautious. They think I don't hear their whispers, but I do.

That's her—that's Delaney Miller. Yeah, she was Dan Hickman's prom date. And she's also the one who got amnesia sophomore year; she was out of school for almost two months. Can you imagine living like that? Going through that much? Maybe some people are just unlucky by nature.

Yeah, maybe they are. And maybe I'm one of them.

So what?

I won't let bad luck dictate my future. I have to keep believing that there's a bright side, that I can find my happy ending. If I can just keep my head up, things are bound to get better eventually.

"It's all going to be okay," I say aloud between bites of chicken.

Tanya smiles—*really* smiles for the first time since we sat down, painting her face as bright as the California beaches where she'll soon be spending her days. "Yeah. You're right. Both of us are stressed, but college is *so* close, and that'll turn our whole lives around. Everything will end up just fine."

It will.

It has to.

Somehow.

chapter two

ONE WEEK LATER

The air is sweltering, far more brutal than I would expect from this late in August—though I don't know how much of it is the weather and how much of it is New York City itself, packed far more densely than I ever anticipated, the streets clogged with sweaty bodies and the reek of vehicle exhaust. Horns blare, street vendors shout, and my driver has his radio volume maxed out. I thought I was ready to handle a big city—I spent eighteen years in Chicago, for Christ's sake—and yet here I am, sweating my skin off in the backseat of an Uber, wondering how exactly anybody manages to live in a place like this.

None of this is doing much to help my anxiety—

And now my phone is ringing.

Again.

I don't even have to look at the name on the screen before I answer.

"No, Mom, I'm not there yet. Yes, I'm staying safe. No, I haven't been kidnapped. Yes, I ate breakfast. Does that cover everything, or should I add something else to the laundry list?"

Her voice is terse through the phone line, and I can picture her all too well: lips pressed into a thin down-turned line, eyes set in a judgmental slant. "You know I don't appreciate that attitude, Delaney."

Yikes. The full name's not a good sign. "I'm sorry, I'm just —it's a lot of stress."

"What's that *awful* music?"

"It's from my driver. Look, I really can't talk right now, but I'll text you once I get to my room, okay?" If the tension in my stomach coils any more tightly, it's gonna cause my whole body to implode.

"Well, that's fine—but I wanted to let you know...."

Her words fade into the background of my attention as we turn the street corner.

Columbia University. An oasis in the grungy hellscape of Manhattan. Ivied, red-brick buildings; emerald green stretches of grass; the domed and pillared Low Memorial Library presiding over it all like a miniature White House.

Now, *this* is more like it.

"I have to run, Mom. I'll talk to you later."

"Laney—"

I end the call and stuff my phone back into my pocket. Whatever she wants, it can wait—because I'm finally fucking *here.*

"Don't worry about it," I tell my driver when he starts to open the door. "I can get my own stuff out."

"If you say so, lady."

I don't just say so; I *know* so. This is it—my first step towards real independence—and I'm gonna seize it by the goddamn horns. I swing out of the car, pop the trunk, and pull out my suitcase, all the while unable to wrestle down a smile. When the driver pulls away, I have to resist jumping in place out of sheer relief.

No more letting people do things for me. No more hiding behind closed doors and curtained windows. I'll take my own suitcase, thank you very much—and I'll start on my own way down the wide walkway towards the registration tables, find my own place in line—

"Ouch!"

"Oh, shit, shit—sorry; I'm so sorry." Embarrassment stings my cheeks as I hastily step backwards. Since when do I get so wrapped up in my own thoughts that I walk right into people? I'm the opposite of clumsy. Hell; I do rock climbing and archery in my spare time—I should know better than to blunder blindly into someone. "Are you okay?"

"I'm just fine. Don't apologize."

What a nice voice, warm and faintly musical. I raise my eyes to the much taller boy that I crashed into—

Oh. Hello.

"Are *you* okay?" he asks, resting a strong hand on my shoulder to steady me.

I'm staring into rich, fawn-colored eyes, twinkling below heavy golden lashes. His face is serious but gentle, with a wide jawline, a swoop of sandy-blonde hair, and a charming, boyish scattering of stubble over his dimpled chin.

"Yeah. I'm great."

He blinks, a questioning smile rising to his lips. "You sure? That was a pretty hard hit."

"Positive." Go figure—my first encounter with a cute guy, and it started with me slamming headfirst into him like a ditz from some crappy rom-com. "I'm just getting my bearings."

"Freshman?" he guesses. "I haven't seen you around."

"Yeah. Delaney Miller, pre-law. I'm from Chicago." I take a deep breath and brush my hair out of my eyes, readjusting my grip on my suitcase.

"Nice to meet you, Delaney Miller. I'm Devin."

Devin—I guess the full name was overkill on my part—is the kind of guy that Tanya would call a *slam-fucking-dunk*. Good-looking, polite by nature, and even decently dressed in a pressed white button-up and tan slacks. If she were here right now, she'd be swooning all over him. I'm less prone to instant infatuation, but there's no denying that this guy is quite something.

"Do you need any help moving in?" His honey-brown eyes sweep down towards my suitcase. "That's not all you brought, is it?"

"My parents are shipping the rest of the stuff. This is just for my first couple of nights." I flash him a smile. "I appreciate the offer, though. Really."

"Hey, anytime. If there's anything else I can do to help you out—I remember being completely overwhelmed when I first came here. Nothing prepares you for how *big* it all is, you know?"

Is that an innuendo? Is he flirting with me? I genuinely can't tell—but, as nice and good-looking as he seems to be, I'm suddenly eager to be on my way. "I've got it covered. But thanks again—and sorry for the whole walking into you thing."

"Don't worry about it. See you around?"

"Yeah—see you."

Taking care to actually look where I'm going, I resume my walk towards the registration area and join the line behind the tent labeled *K-M.*

The sun beats down relentlessly, to the point where even my light green tank top and jean shorts are beginning to feel like too much. Thankfully, I don't have to endure it for long before I'm at the front of the line, across the table from a young redheaded woman in a Columbia University tee.

"Heya." She grins at me, perky and energetic despite the sweltering heat. "Last name?"

"Hi—it's Miller. Delaney Miller."

"Ooh, such a pretty name." She rifles through the basket of manila folders sitting in the basket in front of her. "That's Irish, isn't it? Mine is too—Caoimhe, and you don't even want to know how that's spelled. I keep telling myself I'm going to get it legally changed to K-I-V-A, but the paperwork involved is a total pain." Shaking her head, she hands me a folder with my name and student ID number printed on a white sticker. "This is your room assignment, class schedule, campus map, and key card. You don't want to lose that card—it gives you access to your dorm, the library, the dining hall... everything, basically."

"Got it."

"You're all set, then. I'll get you checked off." She shoots me a double thumbs-up. "Welcome to Columbia, and remember—Go Lions!"

"Go Lions," I echo, stomach swooping in excitement. Soon, I'll be shouting those words from the stands, watching the first of the homecoming sports games—and, after a little while, I might even be hearing them directed towards *me*. I know they've got a good equestrian team here, and while I haven't gone riding since before the car accident, it's one of the few things that I can remember in perfect detail. Here, without my parents to freak out over every single thing that they perceive as dangerous, I'll finally be able to get on a horse again. I can't fucking wait.

Cute guys, school spirit, organized sports... *this* is what life's really about. Not stalkers and strange notes and arranged marriages, but freedom. Real freedom.

And my very own room. John Jay Hall, #316, according to the slip of paper inside of my folder. I was prohibited from locking my door at home, but there's no one to stop me now. Nobody will barge in on me—not my parents, and *definitely* not my creepy stalker. Safety, security, privacy... it's a dream come true.

The campus map easily leads me to John Jay Hall, a looming building of at least ten stories. All three sets of double doors in front are propped open, allowing for a steady stream of students hauling their belongings inside—the looks on their flushed, sweaty faces make me all the more grateful that the majority of my stuff is being shipped. Even if it's still hot as hell when I have to lug all my shit to my dorm, it won't be this crowded.

I follow the flow of the crowd—wide-eyed freshmen, harried parents, bubbly RAs—and find myself crammed against the side of an elevator. Someone's already pushed the button for the third floor. Jesus, there are buttons for *twelve* floors—I don't envy the people who are at the very top.

Thankfully, it doesn't take long at all to reach my floor. I squeeze out alongside a few others, into a long white-walled hall lined on both sides with numbered doors, some of which are propped open by half-unpacked boxes. I edge my way around them, past Room 308, 310, 312, 314...

There. 316. Chest tight with anticipation, I swipe my key card, shoulder open the door—

Wait. This can't be right. There's someone here already. A girl with short black hair, dyed magenta at the tips, and an elfin face currently pinched in concentration.

Thankfully, she doesn't seem to notice me—she's parked

in a desk chair, eyes glued to a laptop computer, with an expensive-looking pair of headphones covering her ears.

I must have gotten the number wrong. I scoot back out, closing the door carefully behind me, and take another look in my folder.

Nope. That definitely says 316, matching the door in front of me.

Great. I'm already stumbling into another awkward situation.

I walk back in, trailing my suitcase behind me, and clear my throat as I approach the girl. She glances up, still with that hyper-focused expression, and gestures for me to wait before returning to her computer.

It's not my intention to snoop, but I can't help noticing her screen—all black, filled with rows of chunky green text. Her fingers dart across the keyboard, typing out several more lines before she finally sits back, pulls off her headphones, and turns to face me fully.

"Yeah?" she asks, raising one pierced eyebrow.

"Uh, hi." God, this is uncomfortable. "So, not to be weird, but I think this is supposed to be my room...? Or maybe they gave me the wrong number, but I don't—"

"This is a double," she says flatly. "I'm your roommate."

Roommate?

Oh, God damn it.

I guess there was never any direct guarantee that I'd be getting a single, but aren't people supposed to be able to *choose* their roommate? I've never seen this girl before in my life—and while I don't like to judge by appearances, she definitely doesn't look like someone I would choose to live with.

"Oh." I force a smile onto my lips and give her a small wave, my other hand tightening around the handle of my suitcase. "Well, hi, then. I'm Delaney, and—"

"Chloe. Pleasure to make your acquaintance and everything. Look, I'm gonna be blunt with you. I *really* wanted to get a single. I'm a compsci major and I need space to focus, so we're gonna have to establish some ground rules. No parties or boys, *ever,* thank you. If you want to listen to music, use headphones. Don't leave the window open; there's a fire escape outside, and any freak could come crawling into it. Keep your shit on your side of the room—clutter disrupts my concentration. And—this is the most important one—do *not* bother me when I'm working."

She utters the whole monologue in one breath. I scramble for a response—I've already forgotten half of the rules that she just barked out. In any case, it's clear that this girl doesn't want to be friends, which is—fine, I guess. It'll be sort of like having my own room after all.

Okay, no. I'm bullshitting myself.

This totally sucks.

But I can at least *try* to make the most of it.

"That all sounds good to me." The smile on my lips feels sticky and fake.

"Great. Thanks for understanding."

And with that, she slides her headphones back over her ears, turns away from me, and gets back to her coding.

Cool. Awesome. What a *warm* welcome.

Maybe she's just in a bad mood or something. I won't let that bring me down—there's plenty else to focus on. The room, for one thing. It's definitely smaller than I would prefer, but at least there are a couple of wide windows in the wall opposite the door. The furniture is divided neatly between the room's left and right sides—maybe it was already like that, but I wouldn't be surprised if it's Chloe's doing. Each of us has a twin-sized bed with a bare mattress, a bookcase, a desk, a dresser... and that's it.

Chloe's boxes sit in a heap on her bed, untouched—I guess her computer took priority over unpacking. The overall impression is a pretty underwhelming one, but surely things will look better once we start settling in, making the place our own.

For now, I pull my suitcase over to my half of the room, leave it beside my bed, and cross over to the nearest window. So, okay, the housing situation kind of sucks, but everything else so far has been perfect. The campus looks just as beautiful from here, and I can't wait to get to know it. The names of the buildings, the best routes to my classrooms, the tastiest dining halls—

My neck prickles.

At first I don't understand what's wrong. Nothing is amiss outside, and Chloe is still busily typing away at her laptop. But my instincts have always been good. Tanya used to joke about how I have a sixth sense. When I start to feel uneasy, there's always a reason.

My gaze sweeps across the view ahead of me. Students, fountains, registration tents, bright green grass...

A cold, sickening chill creeps down my spine.

Someone's looking *back at me.*

I'm sure of it. Between the trees, maybe a dozen yards from the entrance to John Jay Hall. I can't make out his face beneath the dancing shadows of sycamore leaves—and yet I'm somehow sure that it's a man. Standing perfectly still— *unnaturally* still.

No—this is ridiculous. He probably can't even see me. I'm three stories above him, on the other side of a window that's most likely catching the glare of the sunlight. It *feels* like he's watching me, that's all. Despite my best efforts, I've caught some of my parents' paranoia—and I won't indulge it. I won't start seeing ghosts. I refuse.

But, no matter how my mind denies it, the sureness in my gut refuses to budge.

There's somebody there, and he's watching me.

I'm certain of it.

chapter three

The dorm room door bangs open, and I spring straight up in bed, every sense on high alert.

Chloe isn't the type to slam doors. Our past couple of days together have made that much abundantly clear. As I blink the remnants of a mid-afternoon nap out of my eyes, a wild scenario begins to form in my mind: this is the stalker. He *followed me here.* He found a way to break into the room and now—

"Oops, were you sleeping? I'm so sorry!"

That voice is unfamiliar, but it's also not at all intimidating; in fact, the buoyant energy of it reminds me a bit of Tanya. When I finally manage to gather my wits, I see that it belongs to a tall, fit-looking girl with natural curls dyed in a very *un*natural shade of turquoise. She's lingering in the doorway with a guilty smile—and behind her, looking even more disgruntled than usual, is my oh-so-delightful roommate.

"You don't need to apologize to her," Chloe mutters, shouldering her way into the room and closing the door. She stalks to her bed, an unmade nest of black and gray sheets beneath an impressive array of band posters, and flops down without looking in my direction.

The new girl rolls her eyes. "Come on, no need to be rude."

I get to my feet, fingers hastening to untangle a nasty case of bedhead. "Hi, sorry—it's okay. I'm Chloe's roommate. Delaney."

"Dominique—but you can call me Nica." She offers her hand and gives a single warm, firm shake when I grasp it. "I'd normally do the whole intro with my prospective major and all that, but—well, have you *heard?*"

"About your major?" I ask, thoroughly confused.

"About the *attack!*"

"Attack?" I sure as hell don't like the sound of that. Classes aren't even starting until next week, and there are already *attacks* happening? "Like, on campus?"

"Just off campus, technically—but the victim was a student. Captain of the boys' soccer team, super popular—I mean, everyone absolutely loves him, which is why it's so crazy."

It takes a few moments for her words to sink into my still-sleepy mind. "What? That's—Jesus, that's awful."

Nica nods grimly. "Word got out just a couple of hours ago, and now *everyone* knows. He was beaten into a coma. They say he almost *died.*"

"Fuck."

"I know, right?" She doesn't seem all that freaked out, though. If anything, I'm getting the distinctly unsettling impression that she's *excited* by the news of an attempted murder.

"It was probably just some random street bum who jumped him," Chloe calls over from her bed, where she's now scrolling aimlessly through her phone. "There are tons of those in NYC."

"Actually, as someone who *actually* grew up here, Miss Idaho, that's mostly a stereotype." Nica folds her arms and shakes her head, vibrant curls bouncing. "Even if it *was* random, it's pretty freaky. Thank fuck administration isn't calling for a curfew or something—that would be tragic for the party."

"*She* doesn't *know* about the party," Chloe says pointedly. She tosses her phone aside and stands back up. "Come on, let's go to your room instead. Hopefully, *your* roommate isn't in there twenty-four-seven."

Jesus. I don't know what this girl's problem is—as far as I know, I've never done anything to offend her other than just existing. It's not like it's my fault that she got stuck in a double room.

"Sure, sure—" Nica waves her aside. "Delaney, you should totally come. Especially if you've been spending the last couple of days in your dorm. It's healthy to get out and about. Here—give me your number; I'll text you the deets."

I accept her phone automatically when she offers it to me, mind buzzing. They came in here yammering about an attack, and then a party, and now they're accusing me of holing up in my room, which I *haven't* been—I've been exploring the library, the dining halls, the academic buildings; I've even charted out the quickest path to each of my classes. Sure, I haven't really started *meeting* people, but that doesn't make me a lowlife. If anything, Chloe's been the one stuck behind her laptop screen. I don't even know when or how she found the time to make a friend like this.

With my number entered, I hand Nica's phone back; she accepts it with a smile. "Hell yeah. I'll see you there!"

She sounds incredibly confident considering the fact that

I didn't actually agree to come to any party, but I don't have time to correct her before she flounces out the door, Chloe close behind.

The sudden silence rings in my ears. I force myself to take a slow, shaky breath.

That was a lot. I still can't wrap my mind around the first part of what they said. A student was *attacked*—how can they be so nonchalant about that?

Maybe because they don't understand this sort of thing the way that I do. I have to remember that I've got a hell of a lot more experience with violence and trauma than the average girl my age. They don't know what it's like to wake up in the hospital with no recollection of your own name, feeling like nothing more than a bruised bag of bones. They don't know how it feels to be told that your best friend didn't make it, or that your prom date was found dead. For them, it's just another source of gossip—but for me, it's real. Too real.

I grab my phone and type in a quick Google search before I have time to question myself: *Columbia University student attack.*

The results aren't exactly extensive. In fact, even after a minute or two of scrolling, I can only find one hit, and it's on Twitter of all places, from a small account that looks like it belongs to a student.

COLUMBIA UNIVERSITY DOES NOT CARE ABOUT ITS STUDENTS!!! Admin working overtime to cover up a student attack. DON'T LET THEM GET AWAY WITH THIS. @ColumbiaUniversity #DevinLowry

Oh, fuck.

Maybe it's someone else. Another Devin. The name's not exactly uncommon, right? There are thousands and thousands of students on this campus. The odds that the victim might be the very first person that I met when I arrived... they're minuscule. It's practically impossible.

But Nica's words are still burning in my memory:

Captain of the boys' soccer team, super popular—I mean, everyone absolutely loves him...

I haven't used the Facebook app in forever, but that's still the best way I know to find someone by their full name. My hands are trembling as I type in *Devin Lowry,* and I hesitate before hitting *search.*

Do I really want to know whether it's him? Confirming my suspicion will make it real, and that terrifies me. A girl can only believe in so many coincidences.

Nyx. Daniel. Devin. It's like I'm fucking cursed.

But Devin—if he really is the victim—isn't dead. I need to remember that. The hundreds of hours I've spent in therapy taught me a lot of things, and one of them is that the human brain is naturally inclined to see patterns that don't actually exist. Nyx died in a car accident. Daniel was murdered. They aren't connected, even if it feels like they are.

They *can't* be.

Bolstered by these thoughts, I hit the *search* button—

Shit.

It's him.

I don't even need to tap on his profile. The tiny icon on my phone screen is enough to confirm it. That sunny smile isn't something that I could easily forget.

Still not a pattern. That's what Tanya would remind me. It's not healthy to think of myself as being somehow responsible for this shit. The world is a messed-up place, and awful things happen every single minute of every single day.

If I hadn't come here, would Devin still have been attacked?

There's no way to answer that question. No purpose in

dwelling on it. I need a distraction—and, just in time, one arrives in the form of a text message.

> Unknown: Hiii it's Nica!! Party's at 8pm,
> Sigma Chi house. I'll be on the lookout for u!

Screw it. Maybe a party is exactly what I need to get my mind off of things—otherwise I'll be sulking in my room all night long, without even Chloe's silent presence to keep me company. I know myself well enough to predict how badly my thoughts would spiral in that situation.

Instead, I'll put on some makeup, get my ass out of John Jay Hall, find my way to the Sigma Chi fraternity house, and drink a little. Maybe more than a little, but who cares? College is all about going a bit overboard, right? I'll still have a couple of days before the start of classes. Plenty of time to sleep off the hangover.

Another text buzzes my phone. Nica again—or more accurately, *Unknown Number* again. I should add her to my contacts—

Wait.

No. It's not her. This is a different number.

And the message—

My lips go numb.

It's stupid. It's a coincidence. I'm making things up. Half-hearted explanations cycle through the back of my mind, but there's no denying the reality of the words on my screen.

> Unknown: He will never touch you again.

chapter four

Thank *God* I have an excuse to get drunk tonight.

Even now, hours after I deleted the message and blocked the number, I feel sick to my stomach. I don't want to believe it, don't want to even briefly entertain the fact that some creepy fucker followed me here all the way from Chicago—but there's no way to disregard the facts. No matter how many ways I try to frame it, I can't talk myself out of the reality of what happened to Devin.

Not without the lubricant of alcohol, that is.

I know it's not strictly *healthy* to head to a party with the express goal of getting—to put it not-so-delicately—extremely fucking wasted, but it's also not healthy to have a stalker who may or may not be trying to murder every guy who so much as looks in my direction, so I'm willing to cut myself a little slack.

I keep my makeup understated. Mascara and light black liner to emphasize the bright blue of my eyes, a dash of sienna blush at my cheeks and temples, and matte lipstick in my favorite shade, tawny rose. Nica didn't mention anything about dress expectations, so hopefully an aquamarine cami and black skinny jeans will be acceptable.

It turns out that I don't need to worry about finding the Sigma Chi house, because it seems like half the student body is headed in the same direction by the time eight o'clock rolls around, their gossip and laughter filling the crowded New York streets. I follow the flow of partygoers off campus for a few blocks until we reach a series of brownstones, each of them affixed with a gold plaque bearing the letters of their Greek org. Third in the row is **ΣX**—that's my stop.

Okay. First college party. Let's do this.

The entry hall is narrow, and I have to literally shoulder my way past the other students, but I don't mind. There's safety in numbers, right? I'm almost instantly overwhelmed by the heat, the dizzying flashes of LED lights strung across the walls, the hip-hop music pounding loud enough to rattle my bones—and it's a good thing. With so much going on around me, consuming my senses, it's easier to forget.

I squeeze into the living room—

And there it is. A long table set with countless liquor bottles and stacks of red Solo cups, free for the taking.

Bingo.

I dodge past a few dancing couples—well, *dancing* is a pretty generous term for the way they're rubbing up against one another, totally shameless—and grab the nearest bottle. It's about half-full of golden brown liquor, shimmering below the party lights. *Black Velvet,* according to the label. Never heard of it, which probably means it's either dirt cheap or incredibly fancy; considering the venue, I'm willing to bet on the former. No problem. Quality isn't exactly my priority right now.

I unscrew the cap, help myself to a plastic cup, and pour

myself a generous couple of shots or so. Still holding the bottle, I bring the cup to my lips, brace myself, and toss back a long swallow.

Yuck. The taste is bitter and artificial, stinging its way down my throat—but, even as I'm catching my breath, a faint warm glow begins to take root in the back of my head.

Screw it. I pour some more, filling the cup about two-thirds of the way. I've only ever tasted hard liquor before, never had enough to feel much of an effect, and I have no idea how much I'll need to get to a good point—but hopefully this will be enough.

"Delaney! Holy shit! Are you going to drink all that?"

When I turn around, Nica is watching me with comically wide brown eyes, a bottle of beer clutched to her chest. Her outfit is way more revealing than mine—a high crop top and jean shorts, seemingly picked out with the goal of showing as much deep coppery skin as possible—and a flash of self-consciousness passes through me. I stifle it with another hefty sip.

"Jeez, girl." She grins, teeth bright against deep burgundy lipstick. "You really know how to put it back, huh?"

"Sure I do." That's a blatant lie, but she seems almost impressed, and I think I like the feeling.

"Goddamn. Good thing there's plenty to go around." She giggles and takes a swig of her beer. "So, what do you think? How's the party?"

"I just got here, actually."

"Well, what are you waiting for? The backyards where the *real* fun is at—Chloe's out there. Come on, check it out!"

The prospect of seeing Chloe isn't exactly a thrilling one, but whatever. Nica is the closest thing I have to a friend so far, and considering how out of my depth I am, I'll take all the guidance I can get.

She leads me through another jam-packed hall, past a kitchen where at least twenty guys are cheering while one performs a shaky-looking keg stand, and out the back door.

The late-summer air hangs warm and heavy around the throng of dancers and drinkers, heightened with the tang of pot and cigarettes. More string lights—enough to cover a department store Christmas tree—crisscross the fence around the yard, several times brighter than the stars peeking through the New York smog high above. My drink, which I've been steadily nursing, is really starting to take effect now, and I find to my delight that I actually *want* to dance.

"This is so cool!" I half-shout above the thundering music and cascade of voices.

"I know, right?" Nica squeals, beer sloshing out of her bottle as she sways with the rhythm. "Totally lit. I wonder if —" The delight melts from her face, replaced with a shadow of horror. "Oh, my God."

"What? What's wrong?" I try to follow her gaze, but don't see anything out of place, unless you count a couple violently making out against one of the fence posts.

"See that girl? With the dark hair and the bangs? That's Victoria Adelheid. She's *dating* Devin Lowry—you know, the guy who got attacked?"

At first, I can't tell who she's talking about—and, a moment later, I understand why. The girl in the corner looks like she's trying not to be seen. Between her long black hair, her dark turtleneck sweater, and her gray sweatpants, she almost blends in with the silhouette of the tree behind her. Her expression is blank, her eyes distant—and she's holding a mostly empty bottle of vodka. Jesus. I hope she didn't drink all of that on her own.

"I wonder what she's doing here," Nica whisper-shouts in

my ear. "She sure doesn't look like she's in the mood for partying."

I gulp down some more of my drink, ignoring the way that my stomach bucks in slight protest. Nica may be baffled by Victoria's presence, but I think I get it. After all, I'm here, aren't I? And I may not be as upset as she is, but I'm a far cry from cheerful.

"Maybe she's trying to take her mind off of things," I suggest.

"Well, I guess vodka's the way to do it. Yikes. Oh—hey, Chloe!"

Nica peels off from me, and I don't follow her. I can't seem to take my eyes away from Victoria. Nobody's talking to her— or, apart from myself, even looking at her. That seems cruel— she wouldn't have come to a party if she didn't want company, right?

Fuck it. I still feel some responsibility for what happened to Devin. The least I can do is give his poor girlfriend some consolation.

I set off through the pack of dancers, taking more time than I should thanks to a couple of guys whose hands find their way to my waist and shoulders. Beer-soured breath brushes my face, and my ears fill with boozy catcalls—

"Hey, gorgeous!"

"You flying solo tonight?"

"Come on, baby, give us a dance!"

The idea of dancing does sound kind of fun—but now that I've set my sights on Victoria, I can't give it up. I shrug away from the boys' advances, take another hasty sip of liquor, and approach her.

"Hey, um, Victoria?"

She glances up, dark eyes distrustful beneath the harsh line of her bangs. "What do you want?"

Okay, not the friendliest—but I can't blame her for it, considering what she must be going through. "I just wanted to say that I'm sorry. About what happened. If I could have done anything to stop it—"

"Do I know you?"

Ugh. The booze is tugging at my brain, making it tricky to form the right words. "No, but—"

"Then why the fuck are you talking to me?"

My cheeks burn. This isn't how I meant for things to go at all. How can I explain the messed-up way that I may or may not be involved with Devin's attack? "I just—I'm Delaney Miller, and I met him, on my first day—he was really nice to me, so I thought—"

"Thought what? That you and I are on the same level?" Her lip curls with revulsion. "I don't care who you are; you're disgusting. Fuck off. I don't want to talk to you or anyone else."

With that, she flips me her middle finger, tosses back a swill of vodka, and stalks off.

Fuck. Why did I think that was a good idea? And why does part of me still want to go after her?

"Hey, don't worry about her. She's always been a bit of a bitch."

I turn towards the voice and find my eyes locked with those of a much taller guy. He's good-looking in a very different way than Devin, with short-cropped black hair and prominent cheekbones. Before I have time to react, he holds out a hand.

"Harry Cunningham. Quarterback, not that it's a big deal."

"... Delaney Miller."

His grip is warm and firm when I slide my hand into his. "Nice to meet you, beautiful. Anyway, I could convince you to give me a dance? Help take your mind off of that Victoria bitch?"

Oh, to hell with it all. I might as well. "I don't need convincing, actually."

A loose, lazy grin spreads over his face. "Hell yeah. Let's see what you've got."

I'm not a dancer in any sense of the word, but I'm in damn good shape, and it isn't hard to keep pace with Harry as he guides me in a series of swaying steps. His hands are almost big enough to close around my waist, and he's none too gentle with them, pulling me close enough that I can feel the heat emanating from his body.

When the song ends, I lift my cup to my lips—only to realize that it's empty. Jesus, did I really drink all of that as quickly as I did? Might as well grab another one. My head's buzzing pleasantly, but I'm not drunk enough to stop caring entirely. Need to fix that—

But when I try to extricate myself from Harry's grip, he only pulls me closer, until our bodies actually touch.

"Come on, Delaney," he whispers in my ear. "We're just getting started."

The music starts up again before I have time to respond, and—hell—it feels good to dance. I can wait on that drink.

I don't know how long it is before Harry pulls me aside— several songs at least—but as soon as we're at the edge of the yard, away from the kinetic frenzy of the dancing, I'm swept up in a crippling wave of dizziness.

Wow. I brace a hand against the fence to steady myself. The string lights have grown cute, fuzzy little haloes. My heart thuds heavily in my chest, matching the beat of the music.

"You're so fucking hot," Harry hisses in my ear, nudging closer. "Why haven't I seen you around before, huh?"

His hands venture under the hem of my shirt and I stiffen, panic striking me with brief clarity. Hazy as I am, it's hard to tell, but I don't think I want this—then he slides his leg between mine, a hard length straining at my thigh through his pants, and I *know* I don't want this.

"Stop—"

"Come on, we danced so well together... let's have a little fun, baby—"

"No!"

I shove against him, and he stumbles back. His face is a blur. I feel... I don't know... I should lie down. That's a good idea. But I can't. I need to get home. Home... the dorm... I don't know where Chloe went, and I don't want her to see me like this, but I can find my way back, I think.

"Hey, hey. Where are you going?" Harry's voice is sharp and serious when he grabs my upper arm, nowhere near the sickening, sultry purr from a few moments ago.

"Back to my dorm," I mumble.

"Alone? In the streets of New York? At *night?*"

Shit. It does sound stupid when he puts it that way. "My roommate's here somewhere, I think... she can help."

"Hell no." His grip on my arm loosens, but he doesn't let go entirely. "I've got you. I'll walk you back—I went too far just now. This is the least I can do to apologize."

A wasp-like buzzing has begun to drone in my ears. Fuck, I *really* ought to lie down. I don't have time to stand here and argue. "Okay... okay, let's go."

The shapes and colors of the party don't make much sense as he leads me back through the house. At one point, I think someone calls my name, but I can't make out any individuals in the faceless crowd. My stomach is churning, my steps uneven. This is—I'm *drunk;* this is what drunk feels like, and it actually fucking sucks. I don't know what I was thinking, why I decided to have so much... but there *was* a reason, right? There must have been.

Outside again. Harry's got me by the wrist now, pulling me along like a dizzied dog on a leash. The sidewalk is unstable under my feet. I close my eyes, trying to muster some stability—but that only skews my balance further, and I'm actually falling for a second before he catches me with an arm around my waist and pulls me close.

"Easy there," he murmurs. His voice is too close, his breath tickling my ear and spurring an unpleasant shiver that rattles my whole body.

"I need to lie down," I mumble. The words feel too distant, too quiet.

"Yeah, you do. I knew you wanted it..."

What the hell is he talking about? I try to wrestle my fuzzy thoughts together, but it's hopeless. Have we made it back to campus yet? "How much farther?"

"Depends on how eager you are, gorgeous."

He spins me around—my bare shoulders chafe against damp brick, and I'm trapped, trapped between the cold hardness of the wall and the hot hardness of his body. This is wrong—I can't let him—I squirm under his grasp, but he only growls and pushes closer.

"Don't be a whiny bitch—hold fucking still—"

I throw myself to the side with all of my strength. He slips, curses—and I'm in free fall again. Nothing to catch me this time—I barely manage to thrust out my arms in time to keep my head from cracking against the ground. Concrete skins my palms, but the pain is distant, muted.

Somebody's shouting. Maybe more than one person... or else I'm hearing double. I'm *seeing* triple, that's for sure, unable to make sense of the tangle of shadows above and around me. So dizzy...

Arms around me again, lean and strong—but this is a different kind of strength than before. Cooler, smoother... somehow almost familiar.

The ground vanishes beneath me—and, with one final tidal wave of vertigo, so does everything else.

chapter five

Thirsty.

So fucking thirsty. My tongue's three times too big for my mouth, fuzzy and dry. I feel like a raccoon made its burrow in my throat. I squeeze my eyes shut, trying to slip back into blissful unawareness, only to be rewarded with a hard rod of pain through my temples.

And then the nausea comes in a hot, churning wave, souring my mouth and dousing my hairline in beads of cold sweat.

Okay. Hey, God, if you're out there—you can just go ahead and kill me now. That'd be fine.

No such luck. I'm very much alive, and very much awake, and *very* much hungover.

I think that's what this is, anyway. I've never had one before, but this seems to fit the bill—and I sure as hell drank last night. Don't remember how much. I know I tried to talk to that Victoria girl and probably made a complete ass of myself; the memory makes me cringe internally. Thinking I could actually make her feel better about her boyfriend being beaten to a pulp, just because he happened to talk to me *one* time? Real smooth, Delaney.

Then there was the dancing. That guy whose name I can't remember. I started to feel sick, realized I wanted to go home…

After that? Nada.

I crack my eyes open. The light blue shade of my dorm room walls is there to greet me, at least. I guess I made it back… one way or another. I'm even undressed, though I doubt I was in any state to do so myself—my favorite silk nightdress, with nothing underneath.

Swallowing the bile that rises in my throat, I slowly roll over and squint towards the rest of the room. The light from the windows is dishwater gray, casting everything in a gloomy glow—except for Chloe, whose narrow face is, as usual, washed in the blue light of her laptop screen.

She raises her eyes at the sound of my movement. "Oh. You're awake."

"Yeah…" My voice rasps. I cough, and the room spins; when I close my eyes again, I feel like I'm on a roller coaster—but just when I'm sure that I'm going to hurl, the motion subsides, and I'm—well, not *steadied,* but at least a little more in control.

"So, here's the thing." Chloe tilts down her laptop lid and folds her arms, lips pressed tightly together. "When you first got here, I told you that I had some house rules, and you agreed to them."

Oh, fuck. What did I *do* last night? "I'm so sorry if—"

"Nuh-uh. I'm talking."

Whatever. If she wants to monologue, that's her choice. Speaking aloud just makes me feel sicker.

"One of those rules, you might remember, is that you

aren't supposed to bring people back to this room. Especially not creepy-looking men."

Um.

"What?"

"Don't play dumb." She gets to her feet, trudges over to the door, and begins to pull on her black high-top Converse. "You were really fucking drunk, but I'm not going to accept that as an excuse."

"Chloe, I seriously don't remember—"

"Do me a favor and don't bother trying to get your way out of this. I'm not fucking happy. This is about my safety, and it isn't negotiable." She stands up, lays a hand on the doorknob, and shoots one last repulsed look in my direction. "I'll see you later."

"Wait—"

She doesn't wait. The door closes behind her with a firm click of finality, and I sink back onto my pillow, letting out a faint groan.

Well, I guess I'm not cut out for parties.

The hangover's doing me one favor, at least—it makes everything else feel inconsequential. So what if I got a creepy text? So what if a guy from campus got beaten up? At least my damn brain will be working again once I get through this.

First step, water.

I grope at my bedside table, eyes half-shut. God, I hope I filled my water bottle last night. I have a feeling I'm not so lucky, though. No matter how hard I strain, I have *no* fucking idea how I ended up here—probably safe to say that I wasn't worrying about stuff like the coming morning.

My fingers skirt over the wood, seeking the reassurance of cool plastic—

Instead, they find glass.

That doesn't seem right. Frowning, I blink my eyes all the

way open, lean closer, and try to make sense of what the hell I'm looking at.

That's a glass, all right. Full to the brim with water. Next to it, three little white tablets... and a note.

A single piece of plain paper bearing four words in long, slanting script:

Behave.
I'm always watching.

What the fuck?

What kind of creep—is this from the guy I was dancing with last night? A small spark of familiarity lights in the very back of my mind. I *did* let him walk me home, didn't I? The strange man that Chloe mentioned... oh, God. What did I say to him? What did I *do* to him? I can still remember the revolting hardness of his erection when he pressed up against me. I don't think we had sex—surely I'd be sore if we did. I guess I *am* sore, but not down there. I feel more like I took a really nasty fall... and that also stirs at a ghost of a memory, but I can't quite pin it down.

Well, one thing's for sure: I am *not* going to take the unlabeled pills sitting next to the creepy note. Absolutely not.

I can't resist the water, though. When I bring it to my lips, its cool, fresh kiss might just be the best thing I've ever felt. I chug half of it in one go, then pause, wait for my churning stomach to settle, and finish the rest of it.

Now I feel marginally more alive, at least.

Alive enough to be thoroughly freaked out by the note. 'Always watching?' Seriously? If this is a prank, it's one hell of a corny one. Is Chloe the one behind all of this? She's rude, but not *that* mean—at least, I didn't think so.

The pieces fit together, though. Maybe she's even lying about a stranger in the room, just trying to freak me out. Hell, she even has a motive. If she can frighten me off campus, she'll have the room to herself.

That *has* to be it.

Nica might be able to tell me if Chloe's been up to anything suspicious. Unless she's in on it, of course, but my gut insists that she's a good person. Maybe I'm just gullible, but in any case, it can't hurt to ask. If they are working together, my message will serve as a warning that I'm onto their bullshit, and maybe then they'll give it up and leave me in peace.

My phone, to my relieved surprise, is plugged in and fully charged. I open it up to a string of unread text messages from various numbers:

> Mom: How are you? Dad & I miss u tons. Sending love. Call soon please.

> Tanya: Guess who's ALREADY talking to a totally hot Cali guy? He literally SURFBOARDS!!!!! I think I'm in love.

> Nica: Chloe and I are heading back, couldn't find u—have fun!

> Unknown: No more parties, Della. You'll get yourself in trouble.

The phone drops from my hand, bounces off my mattress, and hits the floor.

No. No way. This can't still be happening.

I blocked the fucking number, didn't I? Is this someone else? An extension of Chloe's messed-up prank?

I want to believe that. God, I do.

But I can't. I *know* this isn't her, the same way I know how to eat and sleep and breathe. The understanding is an animal instinct, ingrained deep within my subconscious. Prey recognizing predator.

Not Chloe, not Nica. This is *him*.

The one who sent me the gifts.

Somehow, he really has followed me—or he has a way of spying on me. Regardless of how, he *knows*.

That's not the worst part of it, either.

That name—

Della.

I don't do nicknames. Not since I outgrew 'Laney' at age nine, not that my parents ever stopped using it. The rhythm of my full name feels sophisticated and pretty; why shouldn't I use it?

'Della' feels pretty, too. But nobody calls me that.

Not anymore, anyway.

I wouldn't allow that. It would feel so wrong. Because that nickname only ever belonged on the lips of one boy—lips that have long since ceased to shape any words at all.

Only *he* can call me Della.

Only Nyx.

chapter six

What's dead is dead.

Nothing can change that.

Those words dominate my thoughts over the next couple of days, as the campus hums in anticipation of the start of classes. I try to get out of the dorm as much as possible, but I find myself constantly glancing over my shoulder whenever I'm out in the open, unable to shake the too-familiar feeling of being watched.

What's dead is dead.

Nyx Caballero is gone. It took me a long time to accept that. But it's been years. I've put him behind me.

Do I still miss him? Of course I do. He was my best friend—and when I think back on him, on the cold intensity of his pale gray eyes, I sometimes think that he could have become something more. That if soulmates exist, if I belong with anyone on this planet, it was meant to be Nyx.

That doesn't change the fact that he's dead. I'm never going to see him again, never going to hear those soft syllables in his velveteen voice:

Della.

Sure, it's a stretch to call it a coincidence—but it's *more* than a stretch to imagine that it's anything else. People don't come back from the dead. They just don't. I'm indulging in stupid, childish fantasies. If my life were some kind of romance novel, he would be my happy ending.

But this is reality. Happy endings don't exist, and my dark prince has long since rotted to nothing beneath the earth.

What's dead is dead.

And I cannot let it control me.

"'Whatsoever is, is. It is impossible for the same thing to be and not be.' These are the concepts at the heart of Locke's proposal. Now, you may be thinking, '*Obviously,* Dr. Kassovitz; isn't this supposed to be a *college* course, not a kindergarten lesson?' To which I will reply: You have a *lot* of learning to do, kiddo, so buckle up and prepare to have your mind blown."

A few titters and giggles ripple through the lecture hall, but I'm focused on my notes, fingers pattering away at my laptop keyboard as I try to record the professor's every word. Thankfully, he has a clear voice that carries all the way up from the front of the room, where he's perched on the edge of his desk—a remarkably casual pose for such a distinguished-looking man. Between his tweed suit, wire-frame glasses, and generically handsome face, he's practically a dead ringer for Harrison Ford at the beginning of the first *Indiana Jones* movie. Some of the other girls are dreamy-eyed, but I'm more interested in his lessons than his looks. I always preferred Indy later in the movie, anyway, after he got a bit roughened up around the edges.

So far, Philosophy 101 is easily the most interesting of my classes. American Government was mind-numbingly boring, something made all the more painful by the fact that it started at a brutal eight o'clock in the morning, and Intro to Anthropology was led by a *very* opinionated professor who didn't seem at all interested in healthy debate. Dr. Kassovitz is cool, though—and I can't help feeling that his lesson is particularly pertinent to my current situation.

It is impossible for the same thing to be and not to be.

Plain and simple as that. Just like I've been telling myself—what's dead is dead. Who knew philosophy could be such a comforting subject?

The first day of classes has been a bit grueling, but in the best of ways. I've *needed* this. Settled into the normalcy of a giant lecture hall, immersed in my notes, I can pretend like everything is normal.

"Edward Stillingfleet," Dr. Kassovitz continues, "had no shortage of gripes with Locke's principles. As a matter of fact—"

A knock sounds at the door.

Not one of the two main student entrances at the back of the lecture hall, but the side door just to the left of Kassovitz's desk. He pauses and frowns; a couple of the students whisper among themselves.

Another knock.

"Maybe a lost student?" he suggests, slipping off his desk and onto the floor. "Let's make sure to give them a warm welcome, right? Show them just how much Columbia appreciates—" He glances at his watch. *"Twenty-three* minutes of tardiness?"

Laughter echoes through the room, and Kassovitz is grinning as he pulls the door open—

Until he isn't.

He tosses a glance back towards us, but this time it isn't playful. He murmurs a few brief words to the person on the other side, pauses, then gives a slight nod and gestures with a hand for the unexpected visitor to stay put. Turning towards the sea of wide eyes filling the hall, he clears his throat and calls out a name.

My name.

"Delaney Miller?"

Did I hear that right?

Some of the other students glance at each other. Nobody here knows me by name, and a substantial part of me wants to keep my head down and my mouth shut. Whoever's on the other side of the door, whatever they want with me—I can't let them ruin my first day.

"Is there a Delaney Miller present?" Dr. Kassovitz repeats, and this time there's no mistaking it. He's calling for me—and he sounds urgent.

I raise my hand slowly. His eyes find me quickly, and he beckons me towards the front of the room.

"There's someone here for you, Miss Miller. Feel free to leave your things at your desk."

Now everyone's staring at me. Palms sweating, lips numb, I get to my feet and slowly make my way down the stairs between the desks. Every footfall feels deafening against the polished hardwood.

Something must have happened. Something bad. My parents? My roommate? I hate the way that the latter prospect brings a tickle of relief. I might not like Chloe, but I don't wish harm on people. That's not who I am. Right?

"Sorry about this, Miss Miller," Dr. Kassovitz murmurs when I finally reach his desk. "I'll make sure the rest of this lecture is uploaded online by the end of the day. You'll be excused from the quiz at the end of today's lesson."

I don't *want* that. I want to stay here, want to write my notes and take my quiz just like everyone else—but it's very clear that I don't have a choice.

"Thank you," I say instead. My voice sounds thin and pathetic, but I at least manage to keep my expression composed as I step through the door and into the hall.

Standing there, waiting for me, is a police officer.

My stomach drops to the soles of my feet. I want to go back—but Kassovitz has already closed the door behind me, leaving me alone in this little beige-walled hallway with a man who can't *possibly* have good news for me.

"Hello, ma'am. Thank you for taking the time to speak with me."

Like I had a choice? I stare mutely at him. He's young for a cop, with a black side shave and strikingly full lips—if not for the uniform, I might have thought he was a junior or senior.

"Here. Take a seat." He waves a hand towards the velvet-cushioned bench sitting against one wall.

"What is this about?"

"Please just sit down, ma'am."

Am I in some sort of trouble? My mind jumps to last Friday night, the end of the party that I don't remember, and I sink slowly onto the bench, my pulse racing.

"Thank you. My name is Officer Lu. I'd just like to ask you a few questions."

"Questions?" I echo stupidly.

"That's right. Concerning your whereabouts between ten and twelve o' clock on the night of August twenty-ninth."

Fuck.

"Um... okay."

"I understand that you were attending a party at the Sigma Chi fraternity house four blocks away from campus. Is that correct?"

His voice is gentle enough, but I know better than to open up to a cop. I keep my response brief: "Yes."

"At around ten, you left the party with one Harrison Cunningham."

How the hell does he know that? "Yes. I think so."

"You *think* so?" Lu echoes, raising his eyebrows.

"Yes. I... I had been drinking. Kind of a lot." Maybe that's all this is. Maybe I've been busted for underage drinking—but the party was huge. It's not like I was the only freshman there. Not by a long shot.

"Understandable. You're only young once, right?"

He smiles. I don't.

"Well, listen." He clears his throat, face shifting into awkward solemnity. "I know it may be difficult, but I want you to tell me everything you can remember about your time with Mr. Cunningham, particularly after departing. Please try your very hardest—even the smallest detail could be crucial to our investigation."

"I..." What the hell is happening to me? "I don't understand. Can you at least tell me what you're investigating?"

He grimaces. "It's not a very pleasant matter."

"I don't care. Tell me, or I won't talk." Maybe that's too bold. Too bad. I'm not going to contribute to any sort of investigation blindly.

Lu sighs.

"We haven't disclosed this to the public yet, but I can't legally withhold it from you, so..." He shakes his head. "I'm speaking with you, Miss Morgan, because something very unfortunate has happened."

I wait, heart thudding violently in my ears.

"In the early morning hours of Saturday the thirtieth, Mr. Cunningham was found murdered."

chapter seven

"*Murdered?*" Tanya repeats, her voice squealing with static through the phone line.

"Yeah. That's what the cop said."

"Jesus *Christ,* Delaney. I knew New York was kind of fucked up, but... shit. Are you okay?"

How the hell do I answer that? Of course I'm not okay—and for reasons beyond Harry Cunningham's death. Hell, he's the least of my worries. A small, fierce part of me—a part that remembers how his hardened cock felt through his jeans—is almost glad that he's gone. That he won't ever be able to fill another girl with the dread that his touch inspired in me.

But there's another problem.

Harry, as Officer Lu explained, was found in an alleyway about halfway between the frat house and the school campus. Throat slit, sopping in tacky, half-dried blood, with a couple of infamous NYC rats already helping themselves to his stiffened flesh. They figure he had been dead for several hours at least.

So he couldn't have taken me back to my dorm.

You aren't supposed to bring people back to this room. Espe-cially not creepy-looking men.

If Chloe wasn't lying to freak me out—and, to be fair, that's a pretty substantial *if*—then who the hell was in our room that night?

"De-*la*-ney." Tanya stretches out the middle syllable. "Talk to me, babe."

"Yeah—yeah, I'm okay," I say, hoping that my bright tone isn't too false-sounding. I begin to pace the room, from the window to the door and back again. I don't know how long I have until Chloe gets back from her afternoon class, but every moment on the phone with my friend is a precious one. "It's just crazy, you know? And there's also..."

Shit, I shouldn't. I don't want her to worry. She's probably having the time of her life, soaking up sun in the company of that new surfer boy she texted me about. My burdens aren't hers to bear—and yet she's the only person that I know I can talk to.

"Also what?" Tanya prompts.

"Well—I don't know. It's probably nothing."

"Hm. Now why can I smell bullshit all the way from Cali?"

I roll my eyes, but an unwilling smile rises to my lips, as well. I've missed Tanya and her no-nonsense attitude—more-so, maybe, than I've been letting myself realize. "Okay, so I've been getting some creepy texts."

"Creepy texts? Like what?"

"Just... stuff from unknown numbers. Stuff that makes it sound like somebody's watching me."

"Prank," she says immediately. "Has to be."

"I thought so too, but..." I pause by the window, staring down towards the sycamore trees swaying gently in the breeze. "I don't know. Something about it gives me the ick."

"Listen. You've been dealt a tough fucking hand in your

life so far. Of course you're suspicious of everything. But here's the truth, Delaney: people are assholes. They do all sorts of weird shit for fun. Remember in seventh grade, when that one girl tried to convince everybody that she was a vampire? Now you've got someone trying to convince you that you have a stalker. Same shit, different day."

Sure. Except for the fact that someone is *dead* now. What's that old saying that my mom always used to parrot? *Bad luck comes in threes,* or something like that. Nyx, Daniel, Harry. Three men that saw me at my most vulnerable. Three men whose lives were cut violently short.

And I can't ignore what happened to Devin, either.

I don't say any of that to Tanya, though. Instead, I repeat her words: "Same shit, different day. You're right. Thanks for talking me through this—I know I must be a total bummer right now."

"Nuh-uh. You're just fine. But, hey—if this is really weighing on you, maybe you ought to call your parents."

My reaction is visceral and immediate, filling me with a dread so potent it's almost nauseating. "No."

"Delaney—"

"They'll take any opportunity they can get to bring me home. You *know* that."

"Yeah, but..." She pauses, and I can hear a soft rushing in the background—ocean waves, I bet. I can picture her sprawled out on a beach towel, sunglasses in place, phone jammed to her ear as she patiently waits for me to get my shit together. "From the sound of it, maybe you *should* go home, babe. I know you don't want to hear that, but if you think you're in danger—"

"I'm not." If I end up back in Chicago, I might never leave again. Not just because of my parents, but because of my own misery. Back there, in the place where I lost Nyx and Daniel, it would be all too easy to sink into a lethargic depression, to rot away in my room with the lights off and the windows covered. My only way out would be marriage to that son of a bitch Andrew, who hasn't even crossed my mind since arriving at Columbia.

And I can't live like that.

"You're right—I'm just being paranoid." I take a deep breath and turn my back to the window. "Thanks for the chat. I won't keep you any longer."

"If you're sure you're okay?"

"Promise. Love you."

"Love you too. Toodles!"

She hangs up, leaving me alone.

Except, yet again, some primal instinct warns me that I'm not alone at all.

Tuesday passes without incident, then Wednesday. Classes are unforgiving, and I'm grateful for it; it's hard to worry about ghosts and murders when I'm drowning in hundred-page readings. On the downside, it's also all but impossible to get out and socialize, which is why I find myself turning down Nica's invitation to grab pizza in the city on Thursday night.

Nica: Wish u were here!! The triple pepperoni is to DIE for

Me: Another time, promise

Nica: 🙁

Me: I'm sorry!! I just have so much to do

Nica: No I get it. Good luck kicking that homework's ass

Me: Thanks lol

I don't mention the other reason that I have for hanging back: Chloe's going with Nica and her friends, which means that I actually have the room to myself for a few hours. It's a thousand times easier to focus on my work when my room-mate's erratic keyboard tapping isn't itching at me like a troublesome mosquito.

God, I *am* hungry, though.

I sigh and heave my giant history textbook shut. I feel like I've been rereading the same paragraph for the past hour. Nothing's sinking in. Maybe if I switch to philosophy, my brain will cooperate a bit better. If this is the first week of classes, I can't even imagine how—

Knocking.

My head whips around to stare at the door.

Chloe wouldn't knock—and she's at the restaurant anyway, as is Nica. Who the hell else has any business here? Bizarre possibilities whip through my mind, each of them more absurd than the last—Officer Lu, Victoria, Nyx...

The knock comes again, this time accompanied by a voice: "Delivery!"

Oh, for fuck's sake. I'm getting worked up over nothing again. Someone ordered food, and the restaurant must have messed up the room number. It makes so much sense that I want to smack myself in the forehead. Sometimes, there's a mundane explanation. Not everyone is out to get you, Delaney.

I get up, wincing at the pinpricks in my legs—how long

have I been sitting here, hunched over my desk? I take a moment to stretch, during which a third series of knocks batters the door, then finally walk over to open it.

The person standing on the other side, a skinny girl with a blonde ponytail, looks younger than me. Still in high school, judging by the acne that peppers her high forehead. Her arms are wrapped around a paper bag that looks like it has enough to feed a small army.

"Hi, sorry." I offer a smile that she doesn't return. "Sorry, I think you have the wrong room. I didn't order anything."

"Three-sixteen John Jay Hall?" she checks, sounding even more tired than she looks.

"Yeah, um—maybe they put it in wrong. Is there a name on the order?"

Sighing, she adjusts her grip to get a look at the receipt stapled to the bag.

"Says it's for Della."

My lips go numb.

What the *fuck?*

"Okay. Well." Paralyzed by confusion and more than a little bit of fear, all I can do is respond automatically, mechanically. "I guess that is me, then. How much do I owe you?"

She gives me a strange look, eyes narrowed. "You already paid. In the app?"

Sure. Why the hell not? Things might as well get even fucking weirder now.

"Right, sorry—lots on my mind."

From the way she's staring at me, she probably thinks I'm stoned out of my mind. Between my confusion and the tremendous amount of food, I can hardly blame her for being suspicious.

If only the situation were as simple as that.

I accept the bag from her—Christ, it's even heavier than it

looks—and try my best to smile again. I feel like my face is made of plastic. "Thanks. Have a good night!"

"Uh-huh... you too." Shaking her head, she turns and starts down the hall, leaving me to shoulder the door shut, cross to my desk, and set the bag down on it with a huff of relief.

Think, think, *think*.

Della. That can't be a coincidence. Whoever brought me this is the same person who texted me after the party. The same one, presumably, who left the water and medicine on my nightstand... and, just maybe, the 'creepy-looking man' that Chloe described.

Unless it's all Chloe's own doing, but that's beginning to feel less and less likely. Why would she buy me food? Especially when she's supposed to be out having fun with Nica and their friends? It just doesn't add up. This isn't just spooky stalker behavior—it's almost like I'm being *courted,* in the most bizarre possible way.

Oh, fuck.

That notion—courtship—leads me to a thought so awful that I can barely let myself entertain it.

What if *Andrew* is the one behind all this?

I've always found him to be a pretentious idiot. Annoying, but harmless. Not someone capable of getting his hands dirty.

But he's rich as God, and would have no problem sending some of his family's goons to take Harry and Devin out of the picture.

He could have followed me here. He could be orchestrating this whole demented reign of terror for the sake of the long game. Systematically eliminating everything, as far as he knows, that stands between us and the marriage that our families have planned for us.

It's such a revolting notion that I'm tempted to throw the whole stupid bag in the trash—

But, shit, it *does* smell good. Hot, rich, and spicy; Indian, I think.

Free food is free food, even if it does come from someone I hate. Fuck it—I'll eat it out of spite. If he thinks he's earning himself any favor with me, that's his mistake.

I rip the bag open, and the aroma hits me in a wave so powerful that my saliva glands ache. Three boxes of rice and four plastic containers in total. Palak paneer, tandoori chicken, garlic naan, and lamb korma.

I recognize them, because they're all of my favorite foods.

Andrew doesn't know my favorite foods.

Neither does Chloe.

I check the bag for a note, a clue, anything—but it's definitely empty. The receipt doesn't tell me anything except that the order, paid in full by card, was placed under the name *Della*.

Fuck. I shouldn't eat this. I don't know who would possibly want to poison me, but I shouldn't take the chance… no matter how tantalizing it smells.

My phone vibrates, the buzz loud enough against my desk to make me flinch.

Jesus, I'm getting jumpy. It's just a text message. No big deal.

But even before I lift up the phone, I know in my gut that a text could indeed be a big deal. A very, very big one.

> Unknown: Eat. You need to take care of yourself.

I throw the phone down, leap to my feet, and run over to the window. If someone's out there watching me, I'm going to get a good look at them. My eyes dart across the darkened campus, towards the shadows of the sycamores—

There.

I'm not imagining things. I *know* I'm not. It's there again —the figure that I saw on my very first day at Columbia, tall and slim and inhumanly still. Standing among the trees. I can't make out its face, but I can tell from the tilt of its head that it's staring upwards.

Staring straight at me.

chapter eight

"He was *right there!*" I insist. My voice strains with the effort of holding back tears. "There, by the trees. I swear it."

"Ma'am, I'm going to have to ask you to calm down."

"How the hell am I supposed to be calm?"

The two officers exchange a look for what feels like the hundredth time. Both of them—a tall, heavyset man and a short, skinny woman—have worn expressions of muted exasperation ever since they got here. Even the 911 dispatcher, when I called in a panic, sounded more bored than anything else.

"Let's review this one more time," the woman says, her voice dragging with condescension. "You were studying late, and you'd skipped dinner. Someone bought you takeout. And then, probably after they got the notification that the delivery went through, they texted you from an anonymous number, reminding you to take care of yourself."

"And there were other texts," I remind her. I cast another desperate glance out the window, but of course the silhouette isn't there anymore. It vanished the second that I hung up the call to the police.

"Which you deleted."

"Yeah, because they were *freaking me the hell out!*"

"Ma'am, listen," the male officer sighs, crossing his burly arms. "We're aware that there have been some suspicious incidents around campus lately, but trust me when I say that we see a whole lot worse in this city on a daily basis. Nobody is faulting you for being a little nervous. But the fact of the matter is that nothing is amiss here. My advice? Eat the food, get some rest, and you'll feel a lot more clear-headed in the morning."

"I'm *not* eating that. Shouldn't you take it? As evidence?"

"Evidence of what, exactly?" the woman demands. "Evidence that you have some sort of secret admirer?"

As if things couldn't get any worse, Chloe takes that moment to enter the room.

"Whoa." Her eyes widen as she looks between the three of us. "What happened?"

"Your roommate?" the man guesses.

"Yes, but she wasn't here—"

"Your friend thought she saw something suspicious," he continues, raising his voice over mine. "So she called us in to come take a look. We haven't uncovered any cause for concern—in fact, we were just wrapping things up here. Isn't that right, miss?"

I don't know what to do anymore. I just shake my head.

"All right. You ladies have a pleasant night."

They leave, and I swear I can hear laughter down the hall before Chloe shuts the door and turns to face me, hands on her hips, eyes blazing.

"What the *fuck,* Delaney?"

"I saw something—"

"Nope. I don't even want to hear it." She glowers at the array of food on my desk. "Looks like you treated yourself."

"That isn't—"

"You're fucking weird, you know that? Don't answer. You crossed a *serious* line tonight, and you know it. Pull some shit like this again, and I'm done—I'm getting another room assignment no matter how much of a pain in the ass it is." She stomps over to her dresser, wrenches the door open, and violently pulls out a bath towel and a set of black pajamas. "I'm going to shower. If there are fucking cops or something when I get back this time, I'll..."

She leaves the threat unfinished, exiting the room in a huff.

I slowly sit on the edge of my bed, throat stinging, eyes brimming with tears. Tanya doesn't believe me, Chloe doesn't believe me—even the fucking *police* don't believe me. Where else am I supposed to turn? Nica? What could she possibly do to help?

Bzz. Bzz.

The sound of my phone fills me with dread, but I don't hesitate to pick it up. Why bother? The fucking messages are going to be there no matter what.

Sure enough, there they are. The letters swim before my eyes, but I can still read them all too easily.

> Unknown: Bad girl. You shouldn't have called the police.

> Unknown: Do that again, and I'll have no choice but to punish you.

I can't. I just can't anymore.

I throw my phone to the other side of the mattress, clutch my pillow to my face, and finally let myself cry.

The week crawls by in a blur. No more text messages yet, but that doesn't stop me from shooting awake in the middle of the night, heart racing, mind flooded with scraps of my nightmares: faceless figures, bouquets of belladonna, indistinguishable words whispered in the dark.

Chloe barely talks to me. I get the occasional text from Nica or Tanya, but our conversations never last long. The person who seems most interested in contacting me, of all people, is my mother—I've taken to ignoring her calls, instead opting to text her and ask what's up. She never has much to say.

Not until the end of the second week of September.

Chloe's out again, probably hanging out with Nica, so I've got enough privacy that I *could* pick up the phone—I just don't feel like it. I have a paper due soon for Dr. Kassovitz, so that's a decent enough excuse.

But, a few moments after the ringing ends, my phone gives an extra buzz.

Mom: Call me right now. Urgent.

She found out. That's the conclusion that my mind instantly leaps to. She somehow learned about Harry—or Devin—or, hell, maybe both of them—and now she's going to whisk me back home, back behind the proverbial bars that she and my father have spent their life building around me.

Things will only get worse if I don't call her back.

Shit. Okay. I take a deep breath, brace myself, and hit the dial button.

She picks up on the first ring. "Laney, sweetheart! It's so good to hear your voice!"

I haven't actually said anything yet, but okay, sure. "What's up?"

"That's what I should be asking you! I've barely heard anything about school so far. How are your classes? Your roommate?"

"Good, good." One half-truth and one blatant lie, both of them equally easy to tell. "Mom, can we not do the small talk thing? You said something was urgent."

"Well... yes." She hesitates, and the silence is unbearable. I'm on the verge of begging her to just *spill it already* when she bursts into speech, the words tangled together with excitement. "We were going to keep it a secret, but I don't want to risk it—you can't go making other plans."

"Other plans? What—"

"Andrew is coming to pay you a visit tomorrow!"

Oh, Jesus fucking Christ.

Andrew? *Here?* What an absolute joke—but it's not a joke to her. Not in the least.

"He's flying in overnight," she babbles, "and he's already got the perfect date planned for you two. He's picked out a restaurant and everything—isn't that just the sweetest thing?"

"Mom, I don't know, I'm really busy—"

"Not too busy for Andrew, I certainly hope!" Her voice is still cheery, but it's developed a sharp edge that doesn't escape me. "The two of you have something very special, Laney. You know that."

The only thing I know is that I can't stand the look of his face. Or the sound of his voice. Or his choice of clothes, or his personality, or—

"Laney?"

"I'm here." Though I sure wish I weren't. "I really don't think Andrew and I—"

"Let's not make things unpleasant! You two are going to have a very lovely night together. It'll be nice for you to have a little taste of home. You must feel so lost, all alone out east—"

"It's really not that bad."

"Well, then, this will make it even better." The steely edge is more prominent now, creeping towards the forefront of her tone. "I know you don't like to share much with your father and I, but I'm sure Andrew will be very excited to tell us how everything goes. If he gets the impression that Columbia has been a bad influence on you... we may have to make some reconsiderations."

That's easy enough to translate: *Mess this up, and you're booking a one-way ticket back home, missy.*

"Right. Okay. I understand."

"Good girl." I can almost physically feel her relax, and her next words are perky as ever. "Are you sure you're doing all right, Laney? You sound very tired."

"School is a lot of hard work. As a matter of fact, I ought to get back to studying." Another lie, because I'm sure as hell not going to be able to focus on philosophy after the bombshell that my mom just dropped on me.

"If you say so. You know you can call me whenever you'd like, right, sweetheart?"

"Yeah. I know."

"Okay. Take care. I love you bunches."

"Love you too."

I hang up before she can, turn my phone facedown on my desk, and stare blankly into space.

Andrew is the last thing I need in my life right now.

Especially because I still can't shake the nagging suspicion that he might be the man behind the mask of my mysterious tormentor. In some ways, it makes too much sense—in others, none at all. Whether or not he's a psychopathic stalker, though, I don't want him anywhere near me.

Such a mess, all of it. The messages, the murder, the figure lurking in the shadows—tossing Andrew into the mix is enough to tip me over the edge. My brain is on fire, and my skin feels three sizes too tight, leaving me itchy and restless.

I leave my desk and walk to the window. It's too dark to know whether anyone's looking up at me right now. And so what if they are? I'm not going to let my anxiety keep me from something as simple as fresh air. I unlatch the window and push it open, welcoming the crisp early-autumn breeze that wafts through, layered with the scent of yellowing leaves and city smoke.

One deep breath, then another.

A shower. That's what I need.

I gather my things—towel, pajamas, plastic caddy packed with toiletries—and step out into the hall. Most of the girls on our floor shower in the morning, so hopefully I'll have the shared space to myself.

Sure enough, the tile-floored bathroom is dark and quiet. I carry my things towards the nearest stall without turning on the light. There's something that soothes me about the pairing of hot water and deep shadow, and I could definitely use some soothing right about now.

I turn the handle all the way to the left, and water hisses from the shower head. After shedding my clothes, I test the temperature with my fingertips—perfectly searing.

When I slip inside, the jets spilling onto my shoulders are hot enough to burn, but that's what I want: to burn it all away. My thoughts of Andrew, my memories of the party with Harry, my academic stress... all of it melting into a cloud of heavy steam.

I squirt a small pile of lavender shampoo into my palm, then close my eyes and comb my fingers through my hair, leaning back, savoring the creep of water down my back and breasts, my calves, my thighs. It echoes through the empty bathroom like a perfumed rainfall.

As long as I hold myself together, I'm going to get through this. I always do, right? That's what Nyx would tell me if he were here—that I'm tougher than I look. A born survivor.

We're more alike than they think, Della. You and I... we belong together like the night and the stars.

His words come back to me like that sometimes, in sudden bursts of crystal-clear recollection. Almost like he's still speaking to me now, whispering sweet nothings from beyond the grave.

Times like this, when I feel like I'm on the verge of boiling over, are when I miss him the most. His quiet intensity. The way that, no matter how upset either of us was, his eyes always remained a cool, steady gray.

I'd stay in the shower forever if I could, but it's getting late, and God knows I need some sleep. I'm replenished enough, skin soft and fragrant from my salt scrub and body wash. It'll feel amazing to curl up under my sheets, maybe listen to some music, and just block out the world for a while.

By the time I've toweled up and pulled on my nightgown, my eyelids are sagging. I hope I'm spared from the bad dreams tonight—I've been getting more than my fair share, that's for sure.

There's still a chance that everything will blow over. Maybe the creep harassing me at the beginning of the year has moved on. Andrew, on the other hand—that's a real threat, and hopefully one that I can deal with sooner rather than later. The first step is to endure dinner with him tomorrow. After that? I'll just have to wait and see.

When I close the bedroom door behind me, the window slams shut.

My heart stutters in my chest. "Chloe?" I call, my voice thin—but I know that I'm alone in the darkened room.

Alone *now*.

Moments ago, there may very well have been someone else.

I left the window open. Like a complete idiot. And now...

Maybe it was the wind.

Oh, come on. What am I, a character in some trashy horror movie? There's no way the wind could have done it. Something else is going on, and, screw it, I'm going to find out. I'm done with tricks and secrets.

I reach over to the light switch and flick it on in one firm, decisive motion.

Empty.

My chest heaves, pulse pounding in my ears. The window's shut. Nobody is here.

But when my eyes find my bed, I'm hit with such a violent wave of dizziness that I have to clutch the door frame for support.

I blink several times, but the vision before me doesn't dissipate. My feet carry me slowly towards it, heavy and dream-like, as though I'm moving through molasses. I barely notice when my towel and toiletries slide from my arms and tumble to a heap at my feet.

Belladonna blossoms. Hundreds of them gathered into a rich violet bouquet—freshly harvested, from the look of their tender petals. Their familiar scent fills my nose. Florals and greens, earth and night air.

And the flowers aren't the only thing waiting for me.

A small white card sits in front of them. I know the handwriting on it: the same thin, slanting script that was waiting on my nightstand the morning after the frat party.

That time, there were four words. Now, there are only three.

Remember your promise.

And, taped to the card below the writing...

A ring.

A ring that I *know*.

Dark silver. A braided band inlaid with small, glimmering stones that I somehow know to be black sapphires.

It shouldn't be possible, but...

I've *dreamed* about this ring.

Not nightmares. Good dreams, *enchanting* dreams, brimming with night sky and lake water, with a soft but insistent touch that set my core on fire. Gray eyes, entwined fingers, the ghost of lips along the base of my throat.

Remember your promise.

My promise...

I do remember. Oh, God, I do.

And when I reach out to touch the ring, the memories coalesce into a single soft syllable upon my tongue, traveling to the front of my mouth to the back, a whisper, a plea, a prayer.

"Nyx."

chapter nine

"**W**hat is it?"

"*A promise ring.*"

"*Like... an engagement ring?*"

"*Close. But I like to think it's more than that. If you take this, it doesn't mean that you're agreeing to marry me. It means that you're giving yourself over completely. Swearing yourself to me. Promising to be mine.*"

"*Nyx...*"

"*Do you promise, Della?*"

"*... Of course I do. Of course. You're all I want. All I need.*"

"*Say the words.*"

"*I promise.*"

"*And I promise you, in return, that I will always protect you. You never need to be afraid again, Della. Because you're mine, and nobody, absolutely nobody, lays their hands on what belongs to me.*"

Those words. That night. His touch, his scent.

For hours upon hours, they consume me. I pass in and out

of consciousness, unsure if the things I'm seeing and hearing are dreams or memories. The night feels infinite, and when morning finally comes, I'm afraid. Afraid to open my eyes and find that it was all in my head.

But when I finally muster the courage to glance over at my bedside table, it's still there. Small and bright in the sunlight. A perfect silver circlet.

When I brush my fingers over it, I could swear that it carries a warmth of its own.

This isn't possible.

None of it is.

What's dead is dead.

It is impossible for the same thing to be and not be.

Nobody else knew about the ring, though. Just like nobody else knew about the belladonna... or how nobody else ever called me by that name. Della.

I can't deny it any longer.

Somehow, for reasons that I can't begin to imagine, Nyx is still alive.

Might be alive, anyway. I have to remember that it isn't a certainty; if I let myself believe it entirely, I'll come undone.

The day that my parents told me he was gone... it still hurts like hell to recall. The chemical reek and white walls of the hospital. The way I screamed until I had no voice left. The grave expressions on my parents' faces as they watched me cry, not offering so much as a hug or a word of comfort.

I shouted at them through my tears.

I told them that they were lying. That he couldn't be dead.

Was I *right?*

There's the matter of Nyx's family, too—hell, *everyone* who knew him told me that he was gone.

But nobody knew him quite as well as I did. They thought

I was in denial. They didn't understand that he wouldn't—*couldn't* leave me behind.

I'm drunk with possibility. From the looks that Chloe shoots me from across the room all morning, she thinks I'm *actually* drunk, and I might as well be; I've never felt farther away from the rest of the world. I don't want to eat, don't want to study... all I can do is lie in bed, wound tightly in my blankets, replaying the memories over and over. Good thing today is Saturday, because I don't know how I would bring myself to classes in this state.

When my phone buzzes, excitement flashes through me. If it's him—

It's not.

It's my mother, here to remind me why it's absolutely *not* a good thing that today is Saturday.

Mom: Looking forward to hearing how dinner goes tonight!

Andrew.

Mother. Fucking. Andrew.

The perfect opposite of Nyx. Tan and big-boned, with sweeping blonde hair and teeth that I've always suspected to be artificially whitened. He's a Ken doll come to life, and if I hated him before last night, it's safe to say I *despise* him now.

There's no world in which I'm going to marry that man. Not when I've promised myself to Nyx.

Part of me wants to wear the ring to dinner just to spite him. But I know that would backfire. And even if Nyx is alive, watching me, *wanting* me, I can't count on him to solve all of my problems. Though I can't deny how the thought of him... *disposing* of Andrew, just like I suspect him to have disposed of Daniel and Harry, fills me with a deep, wicked sort of excitement.

Jesus. The guy may be repulsive, but am I really wishing *death* on him?

... Is it so bad if I am?

Is it fucked up that the idea of Andrew at Nyx's mercy, of Nyx's fierce, silvery eyes gleaming as he buries a knife in Andrew's pathetic flesh, fills me with exhilaration... with *desire?*

I shiver and snuggle deeper into my blanket. There's no denying how my body is reacting to the thought. Fuck, I'm actually getting wet, throbbing as I imagine the cool smoke of his voice—

You never should have touched her.

I think it's safe to say that I'm in trouble.

"Are you going to stay in bed all day? Because it's kind of freaking me the fuck out."

Chloe's voice is like a splash of cold water, rousing me none-too-gently from the warm cocoon of my fantasies. I roll over to find her glaring at me, arms folded over a black tank top and a pink plaid skirt, and I'm struck by the bizarre compulsion to burst out laughing—my whole world changed overnight, but my dear old roommate is exactly the same.

"It's Saturday. I'm sleeping in."

"Okay, but you're not actually sleeping, though. You're just... laying there."

"I had a late night."

"*I* had a late night. You were zonked out by the time I got back from Nica's place."

"Is it so hard to believe that it's none of your business?"

Her scowl deepens. "What the fuck's gotten into you?"

What if I told her? *Well, actually, I realized that my child-hood sweetheart—I thought he was just my friend, but I remember everything now—is still alive. He was supposed to have died in a car crash, long story, but he's alive, at least I think he is, and he's been sending me messages and leaving me gifts and maybe even hurting people in my name, to protect me, and—*

"Actually, don't answer that. As long as you aren't on ketamine or something, because room inspections are coming up soon, and I do *not* want to end up in trouble just because you're a weirdo."

"I'm not on drugs, Chloe," I sigh, my fantasies evaporating. "I'm just tired. And I have a date tonight, so—"

"A *date?*" she echoes, her dark eyebrows soaring halfway to her hairline. "Since when do you talk to guys? Or girls? Or *anyone,* for that matter?"

"I thought you didn't care about my business?"

"I don't," she says quickly. "Obviously. I'm just... suspicious."

"Well, be suspicious of someone else. I'm not hiding anything."

She scoffs and turns back to her laptop. "I find *that* hard to believe."

If she thinks the lie is unbelievable, I can't even begin to imagine how she would react to the truth.

At six o' clock on the dot, I receive a text message from a very aptly labeled contact.

> Douchelord Supreme: Hello, sweetheart. I'll be at the front gate of Columbia University in one hour. Can't wait to see you. Wear something nice.

Tonight is going to *suck.*

I've had a little bit of fun getting ready, at least—if only because I've been pretending that somebody very different is taking me out tonight. Andrew will probably find my outfit repulsive, but Nyx would approve—I'm sure of that. A black lace dress with a built-in cami, showing just enough skin to be tantalizing but not distasteful. Heavy winged eyeliner. Matte mahogany lipstick. It's a far cry from my usual understated appearance, and I'm a little bit obsessed with it.

People often say I'm pretty, and it's not that I *don't* believe them—I just don't really see it for myself. As far as I can tell, I look perfectly ordinary, from my dirty blonde hair to my remarkably average C cup breasts.

Not anymore.

Are you watching Nyx? Do you see this? Do you know that I'm doing it for you?

I spend a few minutes trying to brainstorm for my philosophy paper, but it's no use. Between Nyx and Andrew, there's no way I can focus on abstract theories. Besides, that one quote keeps coming up in my notes, and it's enough to make me giddy.

It is impossible for the same thing to be and not be.

Maybe that's what John Locke thought, but I'd bet anything that he never had a long-lost lover return from the dead.

I'm at the front gates at five minutes to seven, my face sculpted into a careful mask of disinterest, pretending not to enjoy the way that pedestrians' heads turn to stare at me. I'm on top of the world, and nothing can bring me down.

A limousine creeps to a halt in front of me, and the back window rolls down.

"Hey there, lovely."

Okay, *almost* nothing.

Between his pearly teeth, golden hair, and blatantly fake

tan, Andrew looks like a parody of wealth. He's dressed to the nines, all the way down to an ugly little lapel pin shaped like a golden rose.

I've never cared for roses.

His lip curls as he looks me up and down. "College has changed you a bit, hm?"

"I'm branching out. Trying new things."

"Huh. I'm not so sure it suits you."

Good thing I'm not looking for your approval, asshole. I force a smile as he opens the door and beckons me in. He scoots partway to the side, leaving me to wedge myself in uncomfortably close, my thigh pressed up close against his. When I pull the door shut, I feel suffocated between it and him, crammed in like a particularly unlucky sardine. Andrew's cologne is bland and over-applied, filling the whole backseat in a stuffy cloud; I have to breathe through my mouth to keep from gagging on the stench.

This is going to be a long night.

"So, I hear you have a restaurant picked out," I say, watching longingly out the window as we pull away from campus.

"*Il Piatto d'Oro.*" He pronounces the name with an exaggerated Italian accent, like spoken cursive. I bite back a cringe. "It's a particularly esteemed venue."

Jesus Christ. Who talks like this? "Cool."

"Come on now, Delaney." His fingers catch my chin and tilt my face in his direction; I force my expression to remain neutral. "Why so aloof? Aren't you happy to see me?"

"I've got a lot on my mind. Classes are hard work."

"Mm." He lets me go, and I have to resist the urge to wipe at the spot where his skin touched mine. It feels dirty, burning. "Art major, yes?"

"Pre-law."

"Oh, dear." He chuckles and shakes his head. "That's a little ambitious, don't you think?"

Keep it together, Delaney. One night, that's all. I just have to make it through this one goddamn night.

"Well, Columbia is a prestigious place. Less than four percent acceptance rate."

"Don't get too boastful, sweetheart. It doesn't look good on you. Columbia is a nice school, yes, but it's far from Ivy League."

Columbia quite literally is an Ivy League member, but I'm willing to bet that he can't name any of them aside from Harvard and Yale. Dartmouth, maybe, if I'm being generous. I shouldn't correct him, but I can't really bring myself to say anything else, either. Instead, I keep my eyes fixed on the window. The gray facades of uptown melt into brighter tones as we enter Little Italy, the limo creeping along at an unbearably slow pace.

"You know, when I said not to be boastful, I didn't mean you should be *quiet*. Sulking is even more unpleasant than bragging."

"I'm not sulking, Andrew." A headache is beginning to lodge itself in my temples. If Nyx were here—but I can't think about Nyx. Not without a physical pang of longing, which feels perversely wrong in Andrew's presence.

"Well, Columbia hasn't made a better conversationalist of you," he mutters. "That's for certain."

"I'm here to study law, not etiquette."

"Careful, Delaney."

I look back at him, and the expression on his face turns my stomach. He's grinning like a dog in search of his next meal, teeth gleaming, eyes blank and humorless.

"You don't want to be smart with me," he says, each word dragged through that awful smile with cold precision. "After all, your parents are very concerned with your performance here out east. If they hear that your manner is growing unpleasant… that might spell trouble for you and your—" He rolls his eyes. *"Legal aspirations."*

I want to knock his stupid fake-white teeth out.

Instead, I coax my face into an expression of mild concern. "That's not very fair, Andrew. I've been working really hard, you know. I'm just tired."

"Well, you really should perk up. Right now, in fact, because this is our stop."

He reaches past me to open the door, grazing his finger-tips none-too-subtly over my chest in the process. I jump out of the limo as soon as I can, but Andrew is behind me an instant later, resting one hand on the small of my back.

"Nice place, don't you think?"

The restaurant in front of us *does* look nice, with ivy-studded walls of sienna brick and tall, black-curtained windows. "It's lovely."

"It's not the only thing. Come along, now."

He ushers me inside, to a wide dining hall full of cande-labras, white tablecloths, and glittering glassware. Soft, romantic string music flows from live musicians at the back of the room. Il Piatto d'Oro is a popular destination tonight; nearly every seat is occupied, but Andrew is unfazed as he approaches the dark-haired hostess.

"Hello, dear. Reservation for two. Clark's the name."

She consults a list atop her podium, then gives a quick nod. "Right this way, sir."

I'm perfectly capable of following her myself, but Andrew seems to be under the impression that I need his hand on my back to guide me. The hostess leads us towards the very back of the restaurant, where a small table sits directly in front of the string quartet.

He smirks as we take our seats. "Pleasant, isn't it? I requested this spot specifically."

"Of course you did."

My words certainly aren't meant as a compliment, but of course he takes them that way anyway.

"Reservations aren't typically made on a per-seat basis, but they made an exception for me. I can be very persuasive."

His *wallet* can be very persuasive, that's for sure. I keep a bland smile glued to my face as a mustached waiter approaches.

"Good evening. Welcome to Il Piatto d'Oro." He sets the leather-backed menu and wine list on the tablecloth before us. "Can I get any drinks started for you, *signore et signorina?*"

His Italian accent is no more authentic than Andrew's. I wonder if this place trains all their wait staff to talk this way.

"We'll have a bottle of your finest red," Andrew declares, not bothering to consult the list.

"Very good. Now, our specials tonight are an angel hair carbonara with guanciale and fresh pecorino romano, as well as a lobster and clam cioppino in tomato-wine broth..."

I tune him out, focusing instead on the slow, dreamy tune of the string quartet. Classical music has never done much for me, but something about the sound now stirs up a strange little fluttering in my chest, a memory of clear gray eyes and black sand beaches, a ring, a promise...

"You're a bit distant, sweetheart. What's on your mind?"

Andrew's cloying tone jolts me roughly from my fantasies. The waiter is gone, I realize, as are our menus. Shit. I must have been more lost in thought than I realized.

"I didn't get to order—"

"You're having the Caesar salad," he says, as though it's the most obvious thing in the world. "Pasta and the like is so fattening, and you're already looking a little out of shape.

All that sitting around and studying takes its toll, I imagine."

Get me. The *fuck*. Out of here.

"I thought the carbonara sounded nice," I mutter.

"Well, then it's a good thing I ordered for you, isn't it?"

I can't even pretend to be grateful. "I'm capable of deciding what I have for dinner, Andrew. I'm not a child."

"You certainly *aren't* a child," he agrees, darting a blatant glance towards my chest. "But children aren't the only ones who need a little guidance now and then. The husband's role—"

"Husband?" Fucking Christ. "Last time I checked, we weren't *married*. Or even dating, for that matter."

Too far.

Andrew's face darkens.

"Oh, please." His voice is sharp and bitter, its sugary lilt gone in an instant. "We both know how this turns out. The least you can do is play along. Do you think I like being paired up with a sniveling bitch like yourself? You're lucky to have that body of yours, because your attitude is downright repulsive. Now shut up, sit back, and enjoy the dinner that *I'm* paying for. Got it?"

My ears ring.

He's never talked to me like this before. Andrew is unpleasant, a complete slimeball—but downright *cruelty* like this? I didn't think he had the spine for it.

I can't marry this man. I've always known that, but this confirms it a thousand times over. I'd rather fucking die.

"Fine," I whisper. "Fine. I'll play along."

And, as swiftly as it appeared, his vicious demeanor is gone, replaced once more by the generic smile that makes my gut churn with its blandness.

"That's my girl. Now, I notice that you haven't asked me

about myself—about how *I've* been—but I'll assume that was just a slip-up on your part. While you've been absorbed in your little studies, *I* took myself on a little tour of Europe. Paris, Berlin, London..."

Thank God for small mercies. This man absolutely loves to talk about himself, and that's exactly what he does for the rest of the evening, regaling me with incredibly dull tales about his expensive vacations. I barely eat, but if he notices, he doesn't seem to have a problem with it—he's too occupied with himself, his food, and his wine, the last of which is gone by the time he pays the bill and walks me back outside.

"You know," he mumbles when we climb into the back seat of the waiting limo, "You *do* have a good body, sweetheart. I wasn't just saying that."

"Thank you," I say tonelessly.

"I *mean* it." He snuggles close, pinning me between himself and the door, reeking of sour grapes. "I was too harsh earlier, wasn't I? We can make this work. We can be good for each other, with a little work..."

"You're drunk," I tell him, shrinking away. I'll open the door and jump out of the damn limo if I have to.

"And *you're* beautiful."

"Andrew..." Shit. The city's night lights are passing far too slowly outside the window. How long is it going to take to get back to campus? I get the feeling that if I resist, he's only going to push me harder. The only thing to do, much as it sickens me, is to feign reciprocation.

"Delaney," he sighs, the breath hot and rancid against my ear.

"We can't do this right now. Not when you're like this." I swallow past the bile building in my throat. "Our first time... it should be special."

"Oh, you're a *romantic*. Fine... fine."

He withdraws, and it takes all of my strength not to let out an audible sigh of relief.

"It *will* be special, Delaney. Very, very special."

He continues to slur out empty promises as the limo makes its way back across the city. I do my best to tune him out, to think about something else, *anything* else, until we finally—*finally*—pull up to the campus gates.

"Goodnight, Andrew. Thanks for dinner."

I don't even wait for the vehicle to stop moving before I'm tumbling out, half-jogging across the grass to put distance between us as quickly as possible. I can't look back. Can't risk seeing his wine-flushed, lust-twisted face again. The only thing on my mind is getting back to my room and locking the door behind me—hell, even seeing Chloe will be a relief.

I've just reached John Jay Hall when my phone vibrates.

Oh—please, *please* let this be what I think it is.

Unknown number.

Thank God.

Maybe I should be frightened. A part of me is, I think—but it's smaller than ever, eclipsed by the much more powerful thrill of my dark desire.

Unknown: Be careful, Della. You know I can't stand to share.

The room is empty when I get back. Chloe must be out late. I'm not complaining—I could use a little bit of solitude after the ordeal with Andrew.

I brush my teeth, wash my face, and change into an oversized T-shirt and panties. After wearing a dress for the past couple of hours, I need something looser than a nightgown. I'm both exhausted and wide awake, fueled by the thoughts that I've been wrestling back all evening.

You know I can't stand to share.

How is it that something so ominous makes me feel so... safe?

No, *safe* isn't the right word. There's an unmistakable thrill of danger to it all. But it's a delicious sort of danger. Irresistible, even.

"Nyx," I murmur, tracing my fingers over the cold pane of the window beside my bed. Is he out there right now, watching me? "Why are you hiding? Why won't you come out of the shadows?"

Maybe because I'm insane. Maybe the stress of all of this —the new school, the text messages, the beating and the murder—has gotten to my head and broken something fundamental.

I might be delusional.

But just in case...

I unlatch the window and push it open, breathing in the rich night air.

"If you want me," I whisper into the dark, "come and get me."

I climb into bed, pull my blanket up to my chin, and drift away with the faintest of smiles lingering upon my lips.

My wrists ache.

That doesn't make sense. Sleeping weirdly on a hand or a shoulder is one thing, but how exactly does somebody end up with a sore *wrist,* let alone two of them?

It's hard to move my fingers, too. They're prickling, half-numb... weak.

The rest of my consciousness swims to the surface, and panic lances through me.

My eyes fly open, only to be met with complete darkness.

Something is wrong.

I'm on my back. I *never* sleep on my back—and my arms are tucked beneath me, straining my shoulders. I can't move my hands. Why the *fuck* can't I move my hands?

"Shh... no struggling, now."

Fuck.

That voice... lower than I remember it, but still velvety smooth, rich and tantalizing.

"You," I whisper past dry lips.

He only chuckles. My eyes strain, but I still can't see a damn thing. It shouldn't be *this* dark. Not unless...

Am I *blindfolded?*

I flinch when a cool, smooth touch caresses the lower hem of my T-shirt, then grasps it and yanks upwards, exposing the whole of my upper body in one swift motion.

This isn't fair. I want to see him—I need to *know.*

Is this another dream? A nightmare? Everything feels so potent: the bite of the cord around my wrists, the thrumming of my pulse in my throat, the spark of wild desire that rushes through me when a hand ghosts over my bare breasts. I can still smell the night air, but there's something else now, too. Black sand and rainwater, dew-kissed violets. Delicate, in a way, with a deep, salty undercurrent suggestive of something far more powerful.

A second hand joins the first, and I can't resist a gasp when he runs his thumbs over the buds of my nipples—not hard, but just enough to tickle, to tease—my back arches, earning me another low laugh.

"I've waited for so long... *too* long," he growls.

"Please—" My heart is like the wings of a hummingbird, beating so fast and light that I'm left dizzy.

"Too many sick bastards, thinking that they have the right to lay their hands on what belongs to *me*. Me and me alone. Promised. Bound."

"Nyx...?" My voice scratches in my throat.

No response. His hands lift away from me, and for a moment I'm awash in panic—I can't let him leave now, not before I know the truth—and, God, *not* while I'm like this, pulsing with desire that radiates from my very core.

But then they're back, sweeping up my thighs this time. My pussy twinges almost unbearably, and my panties are sticky and hot when his fingertips hook around their waistband, pulling them down to my knees.

I whine and buck my hips, desperation beginning to over-take the last traces of rationality in my mind. "Please—*please, I need you.*"

"Need," he repeats—and I can feel his warm breath between my thighs. Fuck, *fuck.*

"Yes—need—"

"What do you know about need, Della?"

His lips brush one inner thigh, then the other. I squirm, whimper as I dilate with aching, vigorous need.

"Do you know..." He nuzzles against each of my hips, taking his time, tasting my skin. "How long... I've needed you?"

"Too long..."

"Much, *much* too long."

I feel him shift above me, and suddenly his mouth is at my ear, licking around the edge, dipping inside until I'm shuddering, eyes rolling back in my head beneath the blindfold. I need him to touch me down there—need it like water, like air, like I've never needed anything before.

"I've done my waiting... years of it, sequestered in the shadows, tortured by my own desire... and you've kept on living your life. You let yourself be touched. You forgot your promise."

"I remember now." A hungry moan bruises my throat. "Please, I—"

His fingers find the point of my pulse where it stutters below my jaw, and then his whole hand spreads over my neck, curling tight at the sides.

"No more talking," he growls. "You *fucked up,* darling Della. And *they* had to pay for it. Their deaths are on *your* conscience, not mine. You killed those men with your carelessness."

I can't reply—he won't let me. The force on my throat is unrelenting—not against my windpipe, but rather the arteries on either side, constricting the blood flow to my brain, blurring my senses. My hearing, my thoughts, the feeling in my extremities... all of it is growing hazy, fading at the edges, leaving me aware of nothing but the coiled, aching desire that consumes my deepest parts—my head is spinning —I realize distantly that if he keeps this up, I'm going to go all the way out—

Then the pressure is gone all at once, and I'm swept up in

such an overwhelming surge of dizziness that I could swear I'm in free fall, that the bed is gone and so is he—no, he *can't* be gone, I need him, *crave* him...

Another touch. A finger at the base of my pussy, swiping ever-so-slowly upwards until it rests against my swollen clit.

Sounds fill the air, deep, sultry moans.

"That's right, sweet girl. That's nice, isn't it?"

God, fuck—those noises are coming from *me*. I roll my hips, desperate for more of him, but he only withdraws his hand.

"You think you understand *need,*" he murmurs. "But you don't. You have *no idea*... how it feels... to let need *consume* you. Transform you. Turn you into an animal."

I *feel* like an animal, thrashing and whining beneath his too-soft touch, pain and pleasure intertwined into a single, throbbing vein of desperation.

When he speaks again, his lips are at my pussy, and I can't hold back a soft, sobbing scream.

"Think of this as a lesson, my Della. *This* is need." His tongue grazes my entrance, flooding me with dizzy sparks. "True need is hell on earth. Torture. That's what you've done all these years... tortured me from afar. Given yourself over to people who have no right to even *look* in your direction. If I truly wanted to punish you... you wouldn't be able to take it. You're lucky I have a soft spot for you."

Too much. If I don't get a release, I'm going to break into pieces. My fingers scrabble at the mattress, but he's tied them too tightly—I can't rip free, can't grab him by the hair and drag him flush against me, forcing our bodies together, thrusting again and again until I'm finally free of this bewitching torment.

Instead, he pulls back *again,* and now there are real tears in my eyes—I'm not built for this, I can't sustain this kind of torture, and if that makes me weak, then so be it; I'll be weak, I'll be subservient, I'll do anything, *anything* for the pleasure to come.

"This," my faceless captor whispers, "is why you *don't break your promises.*"

Something soft and damp closes over my mouth and nose. Startled, I gasp it in—and my head is immediately swept with a fresh wave of dizziness, ears ringing.

No—no. I struggle, twisting beneath him, but the cloth over my face doesn't budge. My awareness is narrowing, and he still hasn't given me satisfaction. I'm still wild with desire... everything's far away, and I'm falling again, deeper and deeper.

Until the darkness consumes me.

"Sweet dreams, Della."

chapter eleven

ungover. Again.

Ugh... really? What's wrong with me? I don't even remember *drinking*.

Andrew polished the whole bottle of wine off at dinner, and I'm sure I didn't have anything after I came back to the room...

Shit. What *happened* when I came back?

I washed up. Changed into my underwear and nightshirt. Propped open the window, got into bed, and then...

Something. Something hazy and confused and flaming hot. A voice, a touch... a dream?

No.

I *know* it was real.

Someone came to me in the night. Restrained me, teased me...

Hard as I try, I can't remember how it ended.

Not with my pleasure. I'm somehow sure of that.

Whatever put me to sleep, it must be the reason why my head is aching like this now.

I should be horrified. Hell, I *am* horrified—in a way. Any

reasonable person would be, and I haven't gone *completely* off the deep end. Not yet.

But if it was him—and it *has* to be him—my ambivalence is nothing compared to my desire.

He wouldn't let me see his face. I was restrained, blindfolded... even the vague, foggy memories are enough to send my heart rate skyrocketing.

I curl in closer on myself beneath my blanket. I don't want to open my eyes and confront the outside world. I want to stay deep in this twisted fantasy, drowning in delicious darkness. Hell, I want Nyx back, but this time I want him to go all the way.

What if he doesn't? What if that was it, the culmination of these months of confusion and fear? A game that he's playing where he doesn't actually plan to give me what I need?

No. I can't believe that. Nyx may be harsh—cruel even—but I refuse to believe that he would leave me.

If death couldn't keep us apart, nothing will.

"What the *fuck* is wrong with you?"

Chloe's voice, ragged with anger, tears me away from my thoughts. I scramble upright, blinking the last traces of sleep out of my eyes, and look over to see her standing in the doorway, clothes rumpled and hair unbrushed, gaping at me like I'm some kind of monster.

"What?" I glance down at myself, but I look normal enough, still dressed in that oversized T-shirt. "I don't—"

"Are you fucking serious?" She closes the door, strides across the room, and points an accusatory finger over my shoulder.

Towards the window.

Which is still open.

Shit.

"Was it like this *all night?*" she demands.

"I just wanted some fresh air—"

"You don't need fresh air when you're fucking sleeping!"

I don't know what to say. She's positively *incensed*, her face dappled with an uneven flush, and I'm barely awake, still wrapped up in the confused memories of last night.

"I told you that I have *rules*, Delaney. *Simple fucking rules.* No men in the room. Don't interrupt me while I'm working. And never leave the goddamn window open. *Anyone* could come up that fire escape, and then what? Didn't you hear about the guy who got killed after the party a few weeks ago? Or were you too wrapped up in your delusional little world to notice?"

"Jesus Christ, I'm sorry!" I throw my hands in the air, equal parts desperate and confused. She's talking about Harry; she must be. She has no idea that me and my 'delusional little world' are *responsible* for his death. "I made a mistake last night, okay? It's not like you were in any danger —you weren't even *here*—"

"What about my stuff? My laptop—do you know how much that thing cost? How much I have stored on it? My entire education, my entire *future,* depends on that hard drive."

"Chloe, nobody's gonna come creeping up the fire escape to steal your fucking laptop, okay? You might be obsessed with your work, but believe it or not, nobody else actually gives a shit."

My words are mean, too mean, but right now I can't bring myself to care. It's all so ridiculous. I'm trying to contend with a murderous psycho who might just be in love with me, and Chloe's worried about her *computer?*

And, hell, maybe I'm a little bit guilty, too. She has no idea that someone *did* come through that window last night. If she had been here, would he have resisted? Or would he have seen her as just another obstacle to dispose of? God, I don't want to imagine that. If I had woken up this morning not to her furious shouts, but instead to the smell of her blood—

"You're insufferable," she spits, tears welling in her eyes. "You have been since day one. Taking up my space, getting the cops involved with your creepy paranoid bullshit, trying to insert yourself into my friendships—"

"Nica *wanted* to be my friend!"

"Keep on telling yourself that. You never even hang out with her. You never hang out with *anyone*—you just mope around all day and toss and turn all night, having your stupid nightmares, and I can't *stand* it any longer!"

The tears spill over and streak down her cheeks. Sniffing, she scrubs at her eyes with the heels of her hands.

I'm dumbstruck. Stupid nightmares?

"Oh, yeah," she hisses, as if answering my silent query. "I know about the nightmares. It's not like you ever shut up. All night long, creepy-ass shit about dead people and flowers—" Her voice breaks into a high-pitched mockery of my own words. "*I know you're watching, I know what you did to them, I know what you want to do to me—*"

Now it's my turn to break into an ugly flush. I've been talking in my sleep, and she never bothered to tell me? How much have I given away? She doesn't seem to suspect that I'm connected to the attack or the murder, but—if this keeps happening, will she figure it out? Will I put myself—or Nyx—in danger?

"Constantly," she continues, "and I'm so fucking *sick* of it. I can't just fuck off to Nica's place whenever you're having a bad night, and I can't *sleep* like this, I can't focus—I can't do anything, and it's all your fucking fault!"

I won't just stand here and take this any longer.

"You don't have any idea what you're talking about," I

snarl. "You don't know what I've been through. Go ahead and think whatever you want about me, but I've always left you alone. I've never messed with your shit. It's not my fault that a guy brought me back here when I was drunk; I don't even *remember* that. I fucked up with the window, I admit that, but—"

Smack.

Hot, bright pain flashes across my cheek. My jaw drops, eyes stinging with tears, and my hand flies to the spot where she—*slapped* me? Is that what just happened?

Chloe looks as shocked as I feel. Her hand is still raised, and she looks from it to me and back again, green eyes stretched wide.

"What the fuck?" I croak through half-numb lips.

"Just—I can't do this. I can't be around you right now."

She whirls around and stomps back out the door, which closes behind her with a decisive thud.

I don't understand.

I was well aware that she didn't like me, but this? The venom in her voice, the spite in her eyes... I've never had anybody *hate* me before. And for what reason? Just because I talk in my sleep and left the window open one time?

The buzz of my phone startles a jump out of me. I lift it from my nightstand and give the screen a cursory glance—

Oh no.

Unknown: She's going to pay for that.

He saw, somehow. Of course he did.

And now he's after Chloe.

I've never replied to any of the texts before, but my hands shake as I hurry to do so now. Wishing harm on monsters like Andrew is one thing, but Chloe isn't a bad person. I wouldn't mind giving her a slap in return—but I don't want her to *die.*

He won't make it quick, either. He said that it was my fault he hurt those men, but I'm sure that at least a part of him enjoyed it. Savored their screams, just as he savored my moans.

God, he's going to rip her apart.

Me: Please don't

Unknown: Nobody lays their hands on you.

Unknown: Nobody but me.

Me: Don't hurt her

Me: I don't want her hurt

Nothing.

Fuck.

I'd warn her, but we never even exchanged numbers. I could text Nica and tell her that her friend is in danger—if I want to look like even more of a crazy person than Chloe already thinks I am.

And, deep down, I know that there's no stopping him. There's nothing that Nica or Chloe or I can do.

When Nyx wants something, he gets it.

You fucked up, darling Della. And they had to pay for it. Their deaths are on your conscience, not mine.

I sink onto my bed and close my eyes, willing myself to think of something—anything—that can help.

I can't. There's nothing. Nyx has shown that he's not afraid to go all the way.

Nyx—

Am I delusional to think that he's the one behind this?

Maybe this is all a paranoid fantasy.

Maybe Nyx Caballero really did die all those years ago, and I'm letting myself be tricked into yearning for a demented stalker who won't hesitate to kill anyone who touches me.

In either case, one thing is for certain.

I'm poisonous. Everyone I dare to love, everyone I'm forced to hate—they're all at his mercy.

He's never going to let me go.

chapter twelve

Me: Hey sorry if this is weird but is Chloe hanging out with u? She hasn't been here all day

Nica: Nope sorry! Haven't seen her since this morning

Shit, shit, *shit.*

The sun has started to set, and I'm officially panicking. Nyx—or, hell, *whoever* my stalker might be—hasn't replied to my increasingly frantic pleas, and now Nica is confirming that she also hasn't heard anything.

I'm running out of ways to rationalize things. My stomach is churning far too rapidly to even consider eating; I haven't had a bite of food since the dinner with Andrew, and I'm getting lightheaded, the room swaying around me as I pace back and forth, back and forth.

Chloe has friends other than Nica, right? Not that I would know, seeing as I never really bothered to ask. It stings to know that she thought—*thinks,* thinks; I can't let myself start imagining her in past tense—that she thinks I'm a total jerk.

And it's even more painful to contemplate the fact that, if my suspicions are correct, I might be something much, much worse than that.

For all intents and purposes, I may very well be a murderer.

I cast a glance towards Chloe's side of the room for what feels like the thousandth time. Her laptop is still there, its power light glowing dull red.

That's a big part of what's scaring me. The computer. She's obsessed with that stupid machine. Leaving it overnight is one thing—even Chloe can't code in her sleep, though I'm sure she wishes she could—but it's been close to eight hours now since she stormed out, leaving her most prized possession alone with someone she despises.

She would come back for it if she could... right?

I drag a hand through my hair, groaning aloud in frustration. What the hell do I *do?* Report her to the school? The police? If she returns later tonight to find cops in her room once again, she'll absolutely lose her shit—the mental image triggers a harsh, hysterical laugh that burns its way up my throat.

How the hell is this what my life has become?

It's dark now, the last amber gleam of sunset extinguished into ashy gray shadow. I don't turn on the light. I'm sure he's watching me already; why bother giving him a better view?

I'm such an idiot. I *wanted* him to come last night, practically invited him in, and now Chloe might be—

My phone, locked in a white-knuckle grip, rumbles with a sudden spurt of vibrations. I don't even process the number on the screen, just tap the green button to accept the call and whip it up to my ear.

"Yes?"

"Well, well, well! Since when do you pick up on the first ring?"

My mother. Shit. I should have known better than to think that Nica or even Chloe would be calling me, ready to give a reasonable explanation for all of this.

Struck by a sudden punch of exhaustion, I sink onto my bed, biting back frustrated tears. "Hi, Mom."

"Laney, baby, you've been *killing* me over here!"

That word turns my stomach. "What are you talking about?"

"Your *date!* Aren't you going to tell me how it went?"

Jesus Christ. The thought of her waiting on the edge of her seat to hear about my stupid date, while I've been agonizing over the all-too-possible murder of my roommate —it's practically comical.

"It went fine," I sigh.

"Well? Juicy details?"

She sounds like an overeager schoolgirl. God—if she cares so much about Andrew, maybe she ought to be the one to marry him.

"There really wasn't anything juicy about it. He took me out to dinner. Told me about his travels. That's all."

"So amazing, isn't it? All those trips he's been on, city-hopping in Europe? You know, your father and I honey-mooned in Paris, and it was the most magical week of my life. I bet Andrew would—"

"Mom, I'm really tired." I probably ought to entertain her rambling a bit longer, just to keep her pacified, but I feel like thirty more seconds of this shit might be enough to make me scream. "Can we talk about this tomorrow or something?"

To my surprise, she doesn't argue: "Well, all right. I'm sure you need some rest after your long night."

"Yeah. Maybe Andrew will have more to tell you." He'll

hate it if she interrogates him, all the more so because he'll be forced to act like he had the best night of his life. He clearly wants this stupid marriage to go through, even if it's only for financial purposes... and because he's apparently interested in me for my body, if nothing else.

"You're not too tired to make jokes, then."

"Wait, what?" I frown towards the room's darkened ceiling.

"He told you, didn't he? I know it was a bit spur of the moment, but..."

"Mom, what are you talking about?"

"The trip. He should have landed by now—though I suppose it depends on whether he was headed for Nassau or George Town."

My head buzzes, and for a moment I feel like I'm about to spill off the mattress. I grab at the blanket, phone slipping aside, trying to regain my balance—

"I wouldn't have thought the Bahamas were his style," my mother continues, "and it's certainly unlike him to leave with such short notice, but—"

"Mom." The syllable is weak and unsteady past my tingling lips. "What are you... what trip?"

"Don't be silly, Laney. I know he told you about it last night. Just before he texted me. It's a shame, really, that he's going to be out of contact for the next few weeks. But never mind all that. Are you playing games with me, young lady? Do you really not remember? Did you get *intoxicated* last night?"

No.

I know two things for sure.

One, I didn't have so much as a sip to drink last night.

Two, Andrew sure as *hell* hasn't gone on an impromptu vacation.

She's still babbling, the words swimming in and out of

coherence below the dizzy hum of my ears. "No wonder you're tired... irresponsible... don't deserve to—"

"Mom, I really have to go. I'm sorry. I'll call you later."

I hang up before she can protest, toss the phone aside, and roll over to bury my face in my pillow.

It's my stalker. It has to be. He's taken Andrew—murdered him, I'm willing to bet—and sent some sort of fake text to my mother to divert suspicion. A fictional vacation to the Bahamas, of all things. It would be funny if it weren't so morbid.

Daniel, Devin, Harry, Chloe, Andrew. It never ends...

And a part of me doesn't want it to.

That's the worst part of it all. I can barely even admit it to myself. All of those people hurt me in one way or another—except for Devin, and I know for sure that he's alive. I don't want Chloe's death on my conscience, but the rest of them? Am I really that sorry to know that they're gone?

This can't keep happening. The consequences will have to catch up with me, eventually.

I don't know what to do. I don't know what to do. I don't know what to do.

It's late, I'm exhausted, and I just want all of this to go away. I want the release that he teased me with last night. If I could reach that height of pleasure, let myself be consumed by the mounting tidal wave of pure sensation, then nothing else would matter. That's the only way that everything could be okay.

Maybe that's what he meant by *need.*

I reach over to my nightstand, and my fingers close around the ring resting there. Its braided band is cool to the touch, though it warms quickly in my grasp.

Without really knowing why, I slip it onto my finger.

Remember your promise.

It might be ridiculous of me, but the ring feels safe somehow. It grounds me. Gives me something tangible to hold onto.

I remember, Nyx. I remember.

I don't know how I manage to fall asleep—but when I do... I dream of velvet lips and black sand beaches, nighttime lake water stretching into a darkly beautiful infinity.

The next morning seems to drag on forever. American Government, Intro to Anthropology, Psych 101—I can't focus on any of them, and it's no small relief when I finally leave my last lecture hall, wanting nothing more than the privacy of my dorm room.

But when I get back, I find that it's far from empty.

"Nica?"

She looks up halfway through stuffing a cardboard box full of Chloe's clothes. Several other boxes sit nearby, some taped shut, some empty; Chloe's desk is bare, and all the drawers in her dresser are pulled out.

"Oh, hey, Delaney." She smiles, but it doesn't quite reach her eyes.

"What the hell are you doing?"

Nica sighs and sits back on her heels, dragging the back of a hand over her forehead. "She didn't tell you?"

"Who—Chloe? Tell me what? Did you figure out where she is?" I kick the door shut behind me and drop my backpack onto the floor—it suddenly feels too heavy to carry for a moment longer.

"Yeah. Yeah, I did." She scoops another armful of T-shirts out of the dresser drawer and dumps them in the box. "She texted me this morning. I assumed she'd told you too, but I suppose she has a lot on her mind."

"Well? What did she say?"

"She dropped out." Nica heaves a sigh, shaking her head. "I guess classes were proving to be too much for her. I knew she was stressed, but... well, apparently it was worse than I thought. It sucks. She was so happy to be here. But not everything works out. Suppose it's good to be humbled by the reminder."

Dropped out? Like hell she did. Her texts to Nica are no more real than Andrew's messages to my mother.

Nyx is working faster. Closing in.

"Delaney? You okay?"

Shit, I'm totally spacing out. I take a deep breath and force myself to focus. "Yeah, sorry. It's just a shock, you know?"

"Tell me about it. It's so weird that she wouldn't tell me face to face. I just got the text, and her room key slid under my door with a request for me to pack up and mail her things. Maybe she was embarrassed, but I wouldn't judge her. I thought she knew that." She shakes her head again, harder, as though she's trying to physically dislodge her confusion. "Well, it's whatever. I'm short a date for this weekend's party now, though. A friend-date," she adds quickly. "Any chance you'd be game?"

"I'm not really feeling up to parties, honestly." Not after what happened last time.

Except...

I can still remember that text message, though it's long

since deleted: *No more parties, Della. You'll get yourself in trouble.*

A spark of rebellion rises in my chest.

Why should I obey him? He's teased me and tormented me, stalked me, hunted me, used and abused me—

And maybe I've had enough.

I need answers. I *need* to know if I'm delusional. Last time I went to a party, I never saw the face of the man who carried me back to my room. But this time, I'll be ready. If I get myself in trouble again—or make him think that I'm going to, anyway—he'll show up. He has to. And if I can lure this son of a bitch out, I can learn whether or not Nyx is alive. For better or for worse, I'll *finally fucking know.*

"Actually, sure. Fuck it. I'll come with you."

Nica's face lights up. "Yeah? Really?"

"Really."

"Yay! Oh, I'm so glad to hear that. I was just going to spend the whole time moping otherwise, honestly. But this'll be good. I could really use a good party."

Are you listening right now, Nyx—or whoever you really are?

I'm breaking your rules. I'm going to a goddamn party no matter what you have to say to me.

Your move.

chapter thirteen

From my stenciled brows to my black high heels, every part of me is begging to be stared at.

I've been planning this outfit all week, ever since I first agreed to accompany Nica to the frat party, and the final product is even better than I imagined.

My ivory silk skirt barely crests my thighs. A stretch of smooth skin spans the distance from my waistband to the hem of a black fishnet crop top. I don't think I've ever been this exposed in public before; even my hair, normally worn at its full shoulder length, is pulled back into a high ponytail that emphasizes the curve of my neck. As for makeup, I've gone the dewy route: shimmery bronze eyeshadow, transparent lip gloss, generous highlight endowing me with an ethereal glow. I look absolutely amazing—and, judging by the glances that I get as Nica and I walk the few blocks to the Sigma Chi frat house, I'm not the only one who thinks so.

I hope you're watching, Nyx. I hope you know that I'm doing this all for you.

I'm not scared anymore. See? You don't need to hide from me.

Whatever you have in store, I'm ready.

Heads turn as soon as Nica and I enter the house. The place is dressed up just like it was for the last party a few weeks ago, down to the flashing string lights and the long table of assorted booze bottles. I can't get as drunk tonight as I did before, that's for sure—but I might as well have a little fun.

Plus, despite my revealing outfit and confident demeanor, I'm still just a little bit nervous.

If I'm wrong about my stalker's identity, and if my disobedience pisses him off too severely...

I may not know his name or his face, not for certain, but I know what he's capable of doing.

I know that I'm risking my life.

Hell, I just don't care anymore. If I'm never going to be free of him, at least I can get some answers.

If I die, I won't be dying ignorant.

Nica, who has no idea how dark and desperate my thoughts have become, offers me a Solo cup and raises one of her own for a toast. "To Chloe!" she declares with a grin, her teeth gleaming under the unnatural glow of the party nights. "Wherever she is now, here's hoping she's a hell of a lot happier there."

"To Chloe," I echo, tipping the rim of my cup against hers.

We drink in unison. My throat stings with unfamiliar liquor—not that Black Velvet stuff from before, but something richer and darker, with an oaky undertone that I actually savor on my tongue.

"Hell yes," Nica giggles. She pours each of us another. "It's best to start out with two, don't you think? Really gets the buzz going."

I probably shouldn't—but if *he* really is watching, this is a perfect way to make sure he's paying attention.

"Why the hell not?"

"That's what I like to hear!" She lifts her cup high in the air. "Cheers to you, Delaney—and to me, and to the rest of the damn school year. It might be off to a shaky start, but things are going to turn around from here on out. I just know it."

I toast and drink. A fuzzy heat takes hold of my temples, paired with a deep, delicious swoop of my stomach.

Things are going to turn around, all right—that's for sure. In one way or another, tonight is when everything changes.

It has to be.

"Delaney? Delaney Miller?"

I glance over my shoulder, only to find the last person that I would have expected to be calling my name—it's that girl. Devon's girlfriend, the one I stupidly approached at the first party. Veronica or something. She looks better than last time —a little more rested, and a *lot* less drunk, with her dark hair and bangs combed to silky perfection.

"Hi, um, sorry...?"

"Victoria," she says quickly, voice straining over the music. "Tori, if you want. Listen, Delaney—I owe you an apology."

An apology? "Hey, no—it's fine. It was my fault."

"Not *that*." A trace of irritation edges her tone, far more in line with her demeanor last time we spoke. "That was an asshole move, yeah. But I... look." She takes a deep breath through clenched teeth. "I did something really shitty. I don't remember a whole lot from that night—but your name stuck with me, and I saw you leaving with Harry Cunningham, and —" She grimaces, and the next words spill out of her in a clumsy jumble. "I tipped off the cops, okay? They came around in the morning asking questions about him, and I was still here, and I was hungover and pissed and said that you looked suspicious."

Oh.

So that's why they singled me out in particular. God—I'd been so caught up in my panic and confusion over Harry's murder that I never even stopped to contemplate how the cops had gotten my name in the first place.

"It was *you?*"

"Yeah," Tori huffs, "and I *hate* apologizing, so don't get used to it. But Chrissy Prescott told me that Hannah Moskowitz told her that Nica Chirunda told *her* that—" She pauses for breath. "That Chloe Summers said you'd been acting weird ever since that night. And it's just been eating away at me, sort of, so... yeah. I'm sorry."

She scowls, as if daring me to reject her apology.

"Well... that's nice of you. Really." I turn back towards the drinks table, hoping that Nica can bail me out of what's becoming an increasingly awkward interaction—but she's melted off into the dancing crowd. Shit. "Um, anyway— how's Devin?"

"Better," Tori says at once, her expression softening when my eyes find hers again. "A lot better. He's—well, I guess he's awake, but he's still really confused. They think he might have permanent damage—"

"Jesus, that's awful."

She shrugs, mouth twisting. "I guess I'm a little bit in denial, but after spending so long thinking he was going to die—I'm just grateful that he recognizes me, you know?"

"Yeah." Guilt burns through me, sharp and acrid. How the hell do I explain to her that it *is* my fault? "I've actually been in a coma before, too. It was really scary, waking up and everything. If his mental state's anything like mine was, I promise that he's beyond grateful to see you."

Tori's eyes widen. She seems to be on the verge of saying something else, biting her lip and glancing back and forth.

After a few moments of hesitation, she ducks in close to me, lowering her voice until I can barely make it out beneath the techno pulse of the music. "You were really in a coma?"

"Yeah. A few years ago, but—"

"Maybe you can help me figure something out, then."

The urgency of her voice cuts through my slight haze of tipsiness, sharpening my attention.

"Figure what out?" I ask, my voice instinctively dropping to match hers.

"He keeps saying weird shit. Mostly in his sleep, but sometimes when he's more alert, too. It's creeping me out, and the doctors can't explain it, but maybe you have some idea of what he's going through. He's so scared, and I feel so bad for not understanding..."

Dread gathers in the pit of my stomach. I don't know what she's about to say, but I'm somehow sure that I don't want to hear it.

"It's nonsense, mostly," Tori continues, chewing harder on her lower lip. "Kind of... childish? But that makes it so much freakier. 'No touching' is the main thing. Over and over, kind of like a mantra, I guess. 'No touching, no touching; I won't touch; he said not to touch.'"

My veins flood with ice.

"I keep telling him that he isn't in danger, but the look on his face when he gets really into it, it's just *terrifying...*"

Her words fade away beneath the buzzing in my ears.

No touching. No touching. I won't touch. He said not to touch.

"I'm sorry," I mumble. Maybe I'm interrupting her, but I can't just stand here and listen any longer. "I don't—I never went through anything like that. I really am so sorry, Tori."

I turn away before she gets the chance to respond, pushing my way through the crowd with no real destination in mind. The writhing bodies and laughing faces around me feel suddenly sinister, as though I'm caught in a knot of cack-ling demons.

He said not to touch.

I'm playing with fire, aren't I? Dressing provocatively on purpose, quite literally, asking for trouble. After Chloe, I should know better. I should know that nobody is safe. If my faceless stalker gets too impatient with me, who's to say he won't take it out on Tori? On Nica, even?

I can't stay here. I'm being selfish, risking the safety of everyone around me in an attempt to sate my stupid, *stupid* curiosity.

It's one thing to put myself in danger. But everyone else?

No. Absolutely not.

Nica might be disappointed if I vanish, but that's fine. She'll be okay. I have to be alone right now.

It takes too long to make my way back to the front door. The two drinks slosh in my stomach, nauseating me. Is he watching right now? Laughing at me as I realize my mistake?

Nyx, or whoever you are—don't hurt anyone else. Please don't. I'm the one you want, and you can take me, damn it. You can use me however you desire, but I can't take the weight of another life on my conscience.

Finally, I manage to squeeze outside, and immediately draw in a gasp of autumn-night air. The chill against my burning cheeks is a relief, but a very short one. The streets of the city are too long and too dark, and he could be anywhere. Lying in wait. Ready to pounce.

Fuck it.

I take off running.

One of my heels breaks almost at once, forcing me into a staggered, limping jog. My breath is a knife in my lungs, ripping through them with every stride.

Away from the party, away from Tori and Nica, away from my innocent classmates.

I barely even register when I've reached the campus grounds. The only destination that matters is John Jay Hall, where I can lock the doors and windows of my room and at least pretend that they'll do something to protect me.

The longer I think, the more frantic I become. What the hell was I thinking, trying to anger him on purpose? What's happening to me? Why am I acting like this?

He's driven me insane.

That's why.

His violence and harassment, his erotic torture, his eerie messages. I'm just an ordinary girl, and he's twisted my trauma to his advantage, disfigured me into someone that even I don't recognize, driven me absolutely wild.

I barrel through the door of my residence hall and pull my shoes off as soon as I hit the carpet. Tears of sheer desperation gather in my eyes as I dash up the stairs to my room—I whirl around, shut the door, and slam the lock.

There.

I pause, gasping for air, hands braced against the door.

Okay. Okay. I'm alive, and I'm alone, and—

Steel-strong arms encircle my midriff.

"You wanted my attention." Hot breath at my ear, tickling, teasing. "Well, Della darling, now you have it."

chapter fourteen

y legs buckle, and I half-swoon into his arms, utterly overcome. He catches me easily, scooping one arm under the crook of my knees and keeping the other at my shoulders, lifting me as though I weigh nothing at all.

Dizzy, desperate. His chest is strong and hot and close—I can feel his skin burning through his thin T-shirt, searing the expanse of bare skin between my crop top and miniskirt.

The hunger takes root at once, blazing in its intensity, drawing a gasp from my lips and a throb from my pussy. Oh, yes. Oh, I needed this back, needed it so fucking badly. The fear, the confusion, the horror, the guilt—all of them are braiding together now, coalescing into a single indescribable emotion that tantalizes and tortures me in equal measure.

Nothing matters. Nothing but this.

He tosses me gracelessly onto the bed. I land with a grunt of alarm, still too weak with shock to pull myself upright—before I can even begin to gather my strength, he's on top of me, straddling me, fingers biting into my waist—I can feel his cock straining against his jeans as he forces our hips together.

"You bad, bad girl," he growls. One hand moves upwards to grip my throat, not pressuring me just yet, but ready to do so at the slightest provocation. "You know what you've been doing. You know how much you've been fucking torturing me, you dirty bitch, you wicked temptress. Della, Della, Della…"

He grinds steadily against me as he speaks—but when I tilt my hips upwards in response, he pulls back. Leaving me squirming and frantic.

Shit.

"Don't you understand?" The hand around my throat tenses, thumb edging at my jawline. "You're *mine,* only mine. Not the other way around. This is my game that we're playing, not yours. And *I* make the rules."

He lowers himself again, gradually, just enough to brush me through the thin barrier of my skirt—and then the silk is ripping as he releases my throat and grips a leg in each hand, forcing them apart. An involuntary keen flies from my lips, and his grip grows tighter, his fingernails cutting harsh half-moons into the soft flesh of my thighs.

"Turn over," he commands. "Now."

I try to flip onto my belly, but I'm not fast enough for his taste. He seizes me by the shoulder and forcibly rolls me until my moans are muffled by the pillow, hands scrambling for a grip on my bed's rumpled sheets.

"Did you save yourself for me, Della?" he demands, wrenching my underwear halfway to my knees. "Are you still a good, tight girl? Do you remember that part of the promise?"

He cups my pussy in one hand, flooding me with a shock-wave of pleasure. I'm already soaking wet, and his fingers are slippery in instants—his low growl of approval makes my head spin.

"Good. Good girl, hungry for your master."

His hand withdraws; I can hear the slickening of his saliva as he sucks my precum from each of his fingers, slowly, seeming to savor every bit of it.

"I could take you now," he rasps, "but that would break your pretty little frame, and broken toys are no fun to play with."

He rakes his nails down the sides of my ass, leaving hot welts in their wake. Oh God, shit—"Fuck me," I whimper into the pillow, "fuck me—"

"What's that, my Della?" He lowers his body over mine, hard heat covering my whole frame, and hisses the words directly into my ear. "What did you say to me?"

"Fuck me," I repeat, squirming, powerless beneath his tight-muscled weight.

"That's not how you talk to me. You know better."

"Fuck me, *please...*"

"That's more like it."

His fingers thread through my hair, tearing it free of its ponytail, ensnaring themselves in its thick locks—he pulls hard, forcing my head up, throat arching as shuddering whimpers of thrilling, delicious pain drip from my lips. Tears well in my eyes, as hot as the blood in my veins—his other hand is between my legs again, fuck, *fuck*—one long, lean finger teases my entrance, then plunges in without warning, startling a scream out of me as I contract around him.

"Oh, yes. Nice and tight, just how I left you." His finger works steadily, pulsing against my shuddering inner walls—it hurts in the most beautiful way, and all I want is more, more of him, more of this, more pain, more pleasure. "Patient now, Della. I need to make sure you're ready."

"I'm ready," I choke out, "I'm—"

He yanks my hair even harder, dissolving my words into a

yelp as white flashes before my eyes like lightning in the darkness.

"Don't talk about things that you don't understand. I've done my time. You can wait a little longer."

A second finger joins the first, this one rougher and more insistent, pushing deeper inside of me. I twist and shiver, powerless as he manipulates me from the inside and outside both at once. I'm liquid beneath his touch, pliable as hot wax. I can feel it again, a blazing coil tightening around my core, carrying me towards the release that I so desperately crave—

And then he's gone. The ache of his absence is immediate and overwhelming—no, no, no, not again, not yet. I can't take any more of this torment, *please*—

Foil rips somewhere above me, a much harsher sound amid our litany of moans and heavy breathing. Oh, God— he's going to do it, that's a condom and I'm going to finally, *finally* get what I need—what I've needed for far, far longer than I ever let myself realize.

"I want you nice and loud for me, Della," he growls, hands at my thighs once again. "I want to hear how much you want this. I want to hear how much you want *me*."

"Yes—oh God, yes, anything—"

Sensation explodes through me as his cock fills me all the way, a hundred times more intense than the two fingers, broad and hard and *fuck,* fuck, this is it, this is what I need, I'm screaming with it—

"Louder." He thrusts sloppily, furiously, gripping my thighs hard enough to bruise, and the thought of those bruises is so unbearably sexy that my throat strains with a scream.

"That's better... I'm going to make you feel so good. Oh, my Della, I'm going to make you feel so fucking good."

Fuck, fuck—he's coming undone. His cool, dark presence,

always so measured, so in control, is unweaving at the seams, exposing the frantic flames of his true self, a storm of raw passion that perfectly matches the desire possessing me.

"So soft. So vulnerable. You've needed this... you've needed me, and you waited, like the good girl you are."

"I waited," I moan, throat straining, "I waited, I kept my promise... mm—"

"No more waiting. No more for either of us." He gasps and grunts, his rhythmic motions becoming faster—it's getting closer, something building to a peak that I *need* to reach, sweet pleasure and scorching pain in equal measure—opposites, in a way, but also the same at their core, burning with equal intensity, just like the two of us, just like him and me.

"Oh God... oh, Nyx..."

"Louder!"

"Nyx!" I scream it out as loud as I can. It doesn't matter who hears because there isn't anyone else, not really, nothing but me and the man that I madly, passionately love with every last drop of my being.

"That's right, Della. Darling, darling Della."

I let myself shatter.

Pure, thundering, heaven-sweet pleasure courses through me in waves, washing the rest of the world away, transporting me to a galaxy of shuddering euphoria. Everything is him, his weight, his heat, his growling, ragged huffs in my ear as he comes along with me—we're moving in perfect sync, hitting that perfect point again and again and again, until I don't know anything else, nothing at all, nothing but him.

The convulsions ease gradually, slowing and softening until we finally come to a halt. I'm boneless, melted from the inside out, limp beneath him.

I've never felt like this. Utter, uncompromised serenity.

This is perfection. This is what I was made for. *Nyx* is what I was made for.

There's just one thing left. The faintest shadow of uncertainty nipping at the edge of my bliss.

"Let me see you," I whisper. My throat is raw, but the words themselves come out clearly enough. "Please. I need to see you."

"... Turn on your back."

His weight shifts as he sits up, pulling away from me. It takes all my strength to haul myself over—my thighs spasm with residual ecstasy when they brush together.

"Okay," I murmur. "I'm ready."

The lamp on my nightstand clicks awake, dousing the room in buttery gold—

And I finally—*finally*—see him.

chapter fifteen

Nyx Caballero looks very different from the boy I once knew, but his eyes are the same. Steely gray, cold at the surface, but burning with a deep, stormy smolder reserved for me and me alone. His features are sharper, leaner; stubble dusts the hard line of his jaw, and black hair hangs over his forehead in a messy tangle. His bare chest, broader than I remember and tight with lean muscle, is a tapestry of tattoos—blades and skulls and belladonna flowers, all black and gray, painting him like the piece of art that I've always known him to be.

He watches me expressionlessly. Silent. Waiting.

"It really is you," I whisper.

"Of course it's me, Della." He holds my gaze without blinking. "You know what I would have to do if anyone else dared to lay a finger on you."

"But you're dead." Sudden tears well in my eyes, and I make no move to fight them. He's so perfect. So fucking beautiful. "They told me you were dead."

"They lied." He raises a hand, and his thumb presses the

corner of my eye, stroking away the tears gathered there. "They lied to keep us apart."

"But—why?" It's not fair. To think that I could have had him all these years, that I could have been spared so much agony, so many nightmares… "We were so good together, Nyx."

"I know. I know." A sardonic smirk curls his lips. "Too good. They weren't happy. Listen, Della… our parents are involved in far more dangerous business than they ever let you know."

"I don't understand."

"I didn't know, either. Not until the attack."

"Attack?" I ask, brows knitted together in confusion. "Nyx, what are you talking about?"

He sighs and closes his eyes. "They told you that it was an accident, I'm sure."

"The car crash?"

"The car crash," he confirms with a grim nod. "You weren't supposed to be in that car with me, Della. A rival of my father's wanted to take me out. You were collateral damage. *You* almost died." His voice deepens to a dangerous growl. "They wouldn't let me see you in the hospital. They wouldn't let me see you at all. Never again, they said. I didn't accept that, so they imprisoned me. Three years in a fucking asylum."

"No." Is that why he's so different now? Hardened by endless days of cruel treatment, locked away from an outside world? He's never been vulnerable, not in the slightest, but there's a new, hard shell to him now that can only be the result of trauma. I should know—I've developed one myself.

"I only thought of you, Della. You kept me alive. Through the beatings, the sedation, the mockery. All of it. I thought of you, and I kept breathing." He swallows hard. "When I finally broke out... when I learned that they'd arranged for you to marry that Andrew Clark *bastard*—" He spits the word out like something poisonous, then takes a second to breathe, shoulders heaving with fury.

"It's okay," I murmur, reaching out to place a hand over his heart. He flinches away at first, then relaxes into my touch bit by bit, his face softening.

"You're right. It is okay. He's not an issue anymore."

"You killed him... didn't you?"

He seems genuinely amused by that—enough to elicit a low chuckle. His tongue runs slowly over his lower lip.

"Yes, I killed him. I killed everyone who dared to hurt you. To touch you, even. Maybe I got a little bit overzealous... but I don't regret it. I made you a promise. To keep you safe. And I don't break my fucking promises, Della."

"... Neither do I." I glance down at my left hand, where the silver ring shines bright as ever. "I can't believe I forgot."

"I would have come to you sooner, but I had to make sure you remembered first. You're different from how you once were. Softer. If I appeared out of nowhere, you would have run."

"No," I object, frowning. "No, Nyx, no—I didn't remember the promises that we made, but I remembered *you*. I missed you. Every single day—hell, every single hour. I felt like I had lost a part of my soul in that crash... I would have come back to you in an instant, if only I knew." The tears are back again; my throat aches. It's all so goddamn unfair. "We could have had so much more time together—"

"We will," he promises, the words rumbling low in his throat. "This is the beginning of our forever."

"But it doesn't work that way! Our parents—the law— you've *murdered* people. And what about the people who targeted you? Your father's rival, or whatever... just because we're together, doesn't mean that we're free. They'll find a way to keep us apart. Real life doesn't have happy endings!"

He watches me calmly as the tears begin to streak down my cheeks. When I dissolve into desperate sobs, he only strokes the side of my face, slowly and tenderly.

"No, darling. There are no happy endings. There are no endings at all."

"What are you talking about? There's *death*—that's pretty damn permanent, right?" My head throbs. "What if they *kill* you, Nyx?"

He laughs at that. The sound is just as soft and velveteen as I remember, drawing a deep, throbbing ache from my chest.

"They already did. And that didn't stop me, did it?"

Before I can reply, he folds his arms around me and draws me close, cradling my head against his shoulder. I can feel the slow, steady beat of his heart through my whole body, and chills pass through me as he brushes his lips over my temple.

"You're mine, Della. Now and forever. We're eternal, my love. They thought death could keep us apart, but it didn't. It didn't. Death, darling, was only the beginning."

THE END FOR NOW...

Want more from Zenna Rose? Turn the page for a sneak peek of Insidious Secrets.

INSIDIOUS SECRETS

Crimson Elite University Book One

ZENNA ROSE

Ever felt like your life was trapped inside a golden prison, molded and manipulated by unseen hands? That's my story —strung up like a puppet, dancing in the shadows of others' desires.

Then, a single letter from my dead mother shatters my gilded cage, revealing a truth too dark to ignore. It leads me to Crimson University, a place shrouded in mystery, where the answers to my past are buried deep. The pull is irresistible, like a siren's call, and nothing can stop me from unearthing the truth.

Except—Ryker Pendragon.

From the moment our eyes meet, he engulfs me, casting a spell with his dark allure. His presence... intoxicating, a magnetic force drawing me into a web of secrets and lies. Every move he makes is a calculated enigma, a dance of danger and desire.

And within the depths of his shadowed eyes, I see a kindred spirit—someone who knows the darkness as intimately as I do. A flame in the night, both a beacon and a warning. Irresistible, yet perilous.

But I have secrets to protect, and a past that won't stay buried. No matter how much his touch ignites my soul, I can't afford to let my guard down.No matter how much he shatters me, I must remain unbroken.

prologue

eople. Fucking. Suck.

Blood drips down my hands, staining the once pristine carpet under my feet as I stare at what remains of my dorm room. I thought coming to this school was what I wanted. To fit in. Be normal. Oh, how wrong I was.

There is no such thing as normal, not for me.

They may think they have broken me...Well. Fuck. Them. All.

chapter one

LIA

THREE MONTHS EALIER

The knife whirls through the air, gleaming beneath the bright Tuscany sun, landing in the wooden target with a heavy *thunk*.

Off-center. Again.

"You're slow today," Emilio notes, dark eyebrows arching. He lounges against a marble pillar on the side of the courtyard, arms folded, watching me with displeased brown eyes. "It's not like you to be lazy, Lia."

"I'm not *lazy*." Clenching my teeth in frustration, I stalk across the grassy yard, seize the knife by its heavy wooden handle, and wrench it free of the target. "Maybe I'm just sick of this stupid bullseye. I thought I was training for self-defense, not some pointless sports competition. I could do better if you brought out the human targets again."

"But we aren't practicing on the human targets today. I told you, this is about *precision*."

I don't hate Emilio—don't even dislike him most days—but God, he can be so *condescending* sometimes. He's in his late thirties, younger than most of the Casa's staff, and yet he talks to me like I'm still a child.

I'm not a child. As of today, I'm eighteen years old—and, after a decade and a half of relentless training, more than capable of taking care of myself.

Emilio's attitude is calculated, intentional; he wants to get me riled up because he knows that I perform better under stress. I'm perfectly aware of that.

But my awareness doesn't make it any less intolerable.

I return to my starting position on the far side of the courtyard and pause, steadying my breathing, focusing. The villa's tall double doors swing open in my peripheral vision, making way for a tall figure in a dark gown that I recognize as Ludovica, the governess.

Great. I guess I've got an audience.

"Remember," Emilio calls, "a steady hand is key. When you get worked up, you give your wrist an extra flick, and that compromises your aim."

"I know," I growl under my breath. Is he trying to make me look like an idiot in front of Ludovica on purpose? Well, it's not going to work. I'll show them both.

Steady, measured. I swing my throwing arm a couple of times, feeling out the weight of the knife, the pressure of the late Italian summer's breeze. Eyes on the bright red bullseye, I ready myself, aim—and throw with my whole body, leaning into the motion as Emilio has taught me, every muscle moving in perfect rhythm to shape the knife's arc.

Thud.

Off-center.

"I've seen better from you," Ludovica observes, stepping forward from the doorway.

Frustration pulses in my ears. I've seen better from myself, too. What's my problem today, anyway?

That's not really a question, though. I know exactly what my problem is.

This isn't just another day of training. Far from it.

My whole life has been leading up to today.

Eighteen years of solitude. Eighteen years of this gilded cage, of the villa's vast, echoing halls. Papa hasn't even bothered to check on me since I was barely a teenager. As far as he's concerned, I have everything I want... and that's true, in a way. Opulent clothes, gourmet foods, top-class personal training in all the most essential areas: fighting, endurance, stealth. My time at Casa Clausura has molded me into the perfect weapon. It's taught me how to *survive*—but it's never taught me how to *live*.

How many nights have I spent staring out my window, past the starlit hills of the countryside, towards the town nestled in the valley below? To me, the golden glow emanating from that huddle of houses is more entrancing than all the constellations in the night sky. There are people down there. Living their normal lives, laughing and dancing and drinking.

People like me, I once thought.

But after all this time, I know the truth.

There's nobody like me.

And, God, I hate it so much.

Papa didn't leave me with zero hope, though. He always promised that, one special day, he would come to retrieve me. That I would finally see something beyond Casa Clausura.

That special day?

My eighteenth birthday.

Today.

That's why Ludovica is here, without a doubt. I predict

the words before they come out of her dry, stiffly held lips: "Your father will be here soon. Dinner is to be served at six o' clock on the dot, and he'll expect you to make yourself presentable. Should you need any assistance—"

"I can get dressed on my own."

Of all the staff and servants that run the Casa, Ludovica is the one who seems to have the hardest time understanding that I'm not a child anymore. In fairness, she hasn't borne witness to the crueler parts of my training—the staged abductions, the torture, the poison—all for the sake of building up my tolerance. Turning me into something as unbreakable as the diamonds that fill my jewelry drawers. Ludovica is concerned with much more trivial affairs. Etiquette and social conduct, mostly. She's taught me, in theory, how to interact with the outside world.

Except that she hasn't. Angelo taught me that much.

Angelo: the delivery man's son. Just a year older than me —but from the way he talked, we may as well have been from different centuries. He and I became friends after I caught him in the library while his father was unloading the groceries. He was hidden within the towering stacks of books —atlases, scientific journals, volumes of world history—but he wasn't reading. He was *playing* with something, a strange little square of glass and metal that he called his *phone.*

I thought he was joking at first. Mocking me for not understanding his little device. I knew what a phone was—at least, I thought I did. Phones had receivers and buttons, and they were for talking to people far away, not for playing games. The thing that Angelo had wasn't allowed at Casa Clausura, and he couldn't fool me into thinking it was some-thing as innocent as a telephone. I was headed out of the library, on my way to report him to Ludovica, when he did something very strange.

He took me by the arm.

The sensation of being touched was so foreign that I couldn't help but freeze. Foreign, but not unwelcome. It felt... warm.

"Wait," he begged me. *"Don't tell them, please. I don't want to get in trouble."*

"Why shouldn't I?" I snapped back. *"If you're just going to make fun of me—"*

"I'm not making fun." His eyes were wide and urgent, deep chocolate brown beneath a tangle of ebony curls. *"Here, please —give me a chance. Let me show you."*

For a reason I didn't dare try to articulate—I know now that it was *curiosity,* a cardinal sin as far as Papa and Ludovica were concerned—I did. I let him show me.

And it was beyond anything I ever could have imagined.

The phone—it *was* a phone; he showed me the number pad where he could make calls—was magical. I still don't have a better word to describe it. That tiny little metal-and-glass device contained pictures, videos, music... and even *games.* Most of them were too difficult for me, having so little experience with tapping on a tiny screen like that, but there was one that I found myself loving. The rules were simple: swap around brightly colored objects to make matching rows and columns. There were other elements to it, like the things that Angelo called 'combos' and 'bonuses,' but I was content enough to spend hours with the most basic mechanics, watching with unceasing wonder as those jewel-bright colors shifted and merged before my eyes.

Angelo laughed at me for that, but it wasn't a cruel laugh. He seemed as delighted to watch as I was to play. Soon enough, we formed a tradition of sorts. Every Friday, when he and his father arrived with the upcoming week's grocery haul, we would huddle in our little corner of the library. I'd play the game, and he'd talk to me—about the town, himself, his friends, his family. About school and computers and television shows. Once, he described going to a concert, and the image that his words painted in my mind nearly brought me to tears. Hundreds of people singing and dancing along as music blasted from a gigantic stage, the air electric with excitement.

Angelo's visits became my most precious hours. I'd spend all week long waiting, and my stomach would grow tight with anticipation at the sound of the doorbell echoing through the walls of the Casa. I finally had something to hold onto. Something to fuel me through the most grueling of training sessions. When I was gagged and handcuffed and waterboarded, gasping for my life against the knife-searing pain in my lungs, I thought of Angelo and the silly little game on his phone, and I endured.

I cared too much.

I got lazy.

Ludovica noticed my change in behavior, and she grew suspicious. It didn't take long for her to put two and two together—and one day, instead of supervising the delivery man as he unloaded, she followed me.

I should have been aware. I was *trained* to be aware. But Angelo and his words, the promise of games and stories, distracted me. I never noticed her watching us, and that was only a further confirmation, in her eyes, that his influence was corrupting me.

There was shouting, crying. I sobbed until the room spun around me, but I couldn't do anything to fix my mistake. The damage was done. After that day, I never saw Angelo or his father again.

I left three things behind that day: my friend, my hope, and my tears.

I locked them away where nobody could touch them. Let my skin turn to steel, my heart to senseless stone. Papa wanted a weapon, and that's what I resolved to give him.

But as my eighteenth birthday began to approach, my defenses started to crack.

And now that the day has come, those cracks are wider than ever.

That's why my aim is off, why my temper is running high. Because I'm finally getting out of this prison of a villa. And while I may never find Angelo again, I'll find *something*.

I have to.

"Young lady!" Ludovica's harsh voice snaps me back to the present. "Are you listening to me?"

She's scowling at me, her lined face drawn tight above her high black collar—I don't know how she tolerates dressing like this in the heat.

"Six o' clock," I recite, "and he's expecting me to look presentable. I understand, *signora.*"

"Good. Now resume your training. I'll be preparing inside."

As soon as the door swings shut behind her, Emilio raises his eyebrows towards me. "Well? Ready to try again, or are you too distracted?"

Heat gathers in my stomach. "Distracted?" I repeat, crossing the courtyard to retrieve my knife. The handle is warm against my palm. "Fine. No more distraction."

I whirl around and hurl the knife as far as I can. It sails through the air, straight as an arrow, and zips past Emilio at eye level, just a hair away from his temple.

He doesn't flinch, just reaches slowly upwards and runs his fingers over his ear. They come away bloody. The scarlet stain is unforgiving beneath the blazing sun.

He smiles.

"Perfect aim. But aim and focus aren't the same, Lia. If you don't learn to focus, you're going to get yourself killed."

With that, he turns around, picks up the knife from the grass, and starts towards the doors of the inner villa.

"You're done for today," he calls back over his shoulder. "Go get yourself ready for your father. You know he doesn't tolerate tardiness."

Download Insidious Secrets today!

about the author

Zenna Rose, a romance author, hails from the lively Chesapeake, VA. When she isn't writing, she's a baking enthusiast and a gardening guru. Laughter till tears? That's totally her style. She's on a mission to spread joy and light up everyone's day. Zenna's all about embracing the unexpected and drawing inspiration from the amazing people around her. And when it's time to relax, she's snuggling up on the couch with her two cats and her ever-energetic dog. They're her ultimate chill crew!

www.zennarosebooks.com